LIES IN ME

LIES IN ME

*Never Accept Anything That
You Never Own . . . .*

ANIS F MALIKI

PARTRIDGE

A Penguin Random House Company

To order additional copies of this book, contact
Toll Free 800 101 2657 (Singapore)
Toll Free 1 800 81 7340 (Malaysia)
orders.singapore@partridgepublishing.com

www.partridgepublishing.com/singapore

DEDICATION

For my mom, dad, my two sassy sisters and also not forget to my friends at *MARA Junior Science College of Jeli* and *High Technical College of Ledang*. To my mom and my dad, thanks for supporting me through all the way. I realize that without both of you, I'll never have courage to publish my first book.

"This is it! This is the peak of my success! Eva! Look what I'd found." "Oh, Professor, you are indeed a brilliant person!" Eva smiles broadly at Professor Henry.

"Well, now all I need to do is announced to my fellow soldiers that we're going to have the perfect heir for this brilliant people. What do you think? Perfectionist will be born in a few decades." Professor Henry takes a quick glance at his computer. He knew that all he needs now is to prepare for the arrival of the genius.

"But, professor…" "You know what I need, right? I need to find more money for the heir. Maybe it will be more useful to prepare as early as we can." As Henry said this, he clicked his tongue.

Eva looks at Henry with a sorrow look. "Even so… We can't guarantee that your experiment is a success." Henry gives his assistant a lopsided smile. "I'm never wrong. And maybe I am not wrong this time."

"What if someone used them to do wrong thing? I mean—your plan doesn't go as well as they must be?" "Eva, please has faith on me." With that, Henry packs all his belonging to start with his mission when someone barges into the lab.

Holding guns, they shouted at them. "STOP! YOU ARE UNDER ARREST!"

CHAPTER I

"You're late again, Mrs. North."
Professor Ren yelled at me.

"Sorry." I bow before taking seat beside Kyle.

"Don't always late. You had missed the most vital things on
Earth every time you are late." Kyle, who got red eyes, with burning
red hair, said. I ogle at him. I don't need his advice right now.

I take out my laptop and start to open '360' document. All about
my researches, all about my 'have to' prowess are in there. Nothing
is ticked yet.

SPORTS:

1) Ice Hockey
2) Baseball
3) Badminton
4) Hockey
5) Tae Kwan Do

MUSIC INSTRUMENTS:

   1)   Violin
   2)   Piano
   3)   Flute
   4)   Cello

LANGUAGES:

   1)   Greece
   2)   Spanish
   3)   Japan
   4)   Thailand
   5)   Persia

All are un-ticked. I take a glance at Kyle's laptop. He had done half of his 'things'. Great!

"What did Professor said before I get into the class?" I asked him, shaking off the nerve in my heart.

"Nothing crucial, just a maze of buildings that you should know as a member of our club—Oops, I mean member of this versatile organization." He replied.

Everyone here in this group is a fast learner, except for me. Suddenly, I realized that Kyle perceives my lappy. Haste, I shut it down. I can feel his unpleasant smirk, and I hate it.

I am in the restroom, thinking about my unseen future when I heard a gossip outside the toilet where I am pondering. What I hate the most is when the 'hot' topic is about ME.

"Have you heard, Stellar? She is no way to go!" Cecelia, one of the ballerina athletes, with long legs starts to talk at my back.

"What do you mean? It's rude to say something like that." Bella, her best chum protested. She is also one of the ballet dancers.

"I knew it, but I can't hold it anymore. I'm the one who suppose to be in 360, not her. Prof. Ken had made a really major mistake in the history of 360." Bella chuckles upon hearing Cecelia's comments with her 'sweet' husky voice. Yeah, right!

"I know how to ice skate, exactly! Hey, and I knew how to speak Spanish and Greece! Don't talk about violin and flute! I am innate with it since I was a baby!" Cecelia starts to boast around her friends.

Bella, the African lady shakes her head while putting her left hand high on hair. "Whoa! Miss. Perfect is back!"

"I am not trying to promote myself, but I think I am better than Stellar! Kyle just told me that all the things that Stellar should prowess at, still un-ticked. Which mean, she doesn't even get the basic at all?"

"Well, maybe Prof. Ken will consider his choice later on. Which mean you still have a chance?" Julia, another best buddy, added. She is always by the blonde Cecelia's side.

I push the toilet's door until it slam onto the mosaic wall. "You can take my position if you want! 360 is suck!" After I yelled at them, I hurriedly left the washroom. I don't care anymore. I hate to be in the group. I feel like a stupid kid in there who are inept in everything that I did. I told dad hundred times about it, but, will he listen to me?

"Come in, Mrs. North." Prof. Ken invited me in after I knock several time.

I pull my sleeves longer until my fingers are all covered in my gray sleeves. I play a little bit with my tousle black hair while Prof. Ken is still ignoring me. When are you going to let me sit, Prof?

Suddenly, he held out his hand. At last—
But, then he shows his index finger—which mean halt. What is he trying to say?

"Prof, I need to talk. We—need to talk." I sway my hands from me to him and to me back. That's when he lifts up his chin and gives that absurd smile to me. "Yes, of course, Mrs. North. That's why you are here." I force myself to smile. This is awkward.

"It's about 360,"
"Don't tell me. I got it."
I sigh. What a cold old man.
"You can't quit." "WHAT? WHY? W—WH…"

"Zip it. Whatever you do, you will never quit."
"Prof, you see my report card, right? I wasn't doing things correctly since I was thrown into this creepy group! And, I don't know how to catch up. Those cryptic kids in the groups, they are just too fast." I explained the real situation.

I scoffed, now I really had to face the risk. "There's a girl who is really good in everything. She really wants to be in this group."

"We don't take students with excessive desire. We take students who are good." Hearing Prof. Ken's words make me burning inside.
"Then, tell me what am I good at? I never walked in to the test to be in here. I never want this! I don't want to be a perfectionist.

All I know is I like to dance and that's why I'm a cheerleader before, and I exactly know everything about updated fashions!"

I stand up harshly from the chair in front of Prof. Ken's desk. He just lets me leave. That's disgust me! Acting like everything is okay and pretend that I don't exist. I bang his office door. When I peek at the glass window, he never flinches, locking his eyes onto the screen monitor. THIS IS UNBELIEVABLE!!!

CHAPTER II

"I heard you slamming."

I take a step backward. It's Zen. Zen O'Carter, one of the '360' group, same as me but only that he is three years older than me. "You scared me," I said.

I perceive him playing his cubic. His hand is so strong, deft and—lot of veins. He's pretty tall, with shiny black hair. His eyes are a bit red, crimson is what I meant. What I notice the most is that he likes to wear a dark green fingerless leather glove with a round neck shirt.

"It's rude to stare." He chuckles while I am blushing. "Sorry," I apologized half whispering.

"I heard you try so hard to quit. Well, try harder next time. See ya," with the last word, he runs away from the hallway, locking his eyes on his cubic. I sigh.

"MRS. NORTH, WILL YOU WAKE UP!"

Sheesh!!! Everyone is laughing at me. This is not supposed to happen. I scratch my ears when Prof. Anora, my Greece lecturer yelled absolutely at my ears.

Why am I feeling like I am in high school? Come on, guys! We are in the university right now.

I am in Greece lesson, trying to catch up with those lesson, I fell asleep. The professor should be ignoring me, but since I am one of the most university's prior assets, she mustn't let me sleep and make me focus in every single detail that she said.

"Mrs. North, please write me a 10 pages essay of 'Why I Like to Sleep in Greece Class?' and 'The Interesting Story about Greece Language That I Like'. I'll be expecting it by tomorrow morning, before 9, on my desk! Understood?"

Lazily, I put my side bag on my left shoulder and about to leave when professor called me out, "And make it in Greece!" What the— Ughh!!! I hate Greece!

It's so picturesque. The orange sky, with half blood color make it seems so scenery. The wind that is blowing really relish my mind, I feel grateful. No more problems to think about.

I look down and watch the sea, greenish-blue. After a while, I stand up on the giant rock and scream out of my lung.

I scream so hard that I close my eyes. I scream so hard that I think that my ears can't bear my voice. I scream so hard that my head feel dizzy. I scream so hard that—someone told me to hush.

THAT'S RUDE! I turn around to see a man, shirtless with boxer frowning at me.

"You made my dog ran away, thanks!" (Sarcastic)

James is putting on the fire. The breezy beach wind is so chilling! I hadn't change my morning shirt yet, and I don't step foot in my home yet. I just feel like I don't want to.

"You shouldn't run away from home," James accused. "I am not running away. I was just having some time out here." Because of me, I had to find James' dog all evening. Its name is Kimble. Finding him is like looking for an ant in sugar. It is unbelievably tough. I swear not to scream anymore when animals are around.

James had this tousle blond hair with red eyes, very natural. Beardless, he hates hair on his body. I just knew him yet I describe him like I was his pal for more than 10 years. He owns a villa around the beach, and it's pretty posh. His dad is around, watching him and teach him on how to manage the villa. He also paints. Well, he likes it though *(that's what he said to me)*.

"So, about 360, it's kind of fun game." James said.

"It's not a game! It's a group, to born perfectionists in the university. It is obviously absurd!" "Sounds like fun to me! Hey, it's kind of advantages to a lot of people. The member, the university, the society…"

I gape. Why is everybody thinks that 360 group is lot of fun? All that we did is learn, learn and learn.

"Listen, James. 360 group trained all day, all night, every single hour, minute, second; we trained to be very prowess at the things that we have to." "Like…"

"We need to master 5 sports, 5 languages and 4 music instruments, each of us." "Then, what happened when you are good at them?" James asked with interest.

"They'll use us when they needed. In every match, 360 is the most prior person in the game because we are prowess in it. We are like a machine, winning all the matches for school. In orchestra, we will win because we are the master. University will has masters in each of the music instruments. In language, we are like robots, translating every single word, every single day."

"What are you translating?"

I shrug and shake my head. "I don't know. I never pass the test. I had never been brought into any matches yet. And I hadn't been in school's orchestra yet." I look at my bare feet. "I am suck." I complaint. James smiled.

"I know that you really want to be in the group. But, you are afraid because you are not like them."

James' words make me sick.

"Then, why they chose me in the first place? Everybody had always respected and looked high on 360 groups. They are like—the champion of the school. But, they never look at me like the way they look at other 360." James bites his bottom lip.

"I think you need to practice thrice harder than them. You are deadly good." "We just met and you told me that? Aww so sweet." I said contently. Suddenly, Kimble comes and keeps sticking at James. "Hey, buddy. Aren't sleeping yet? Are you hungry? Do you want some meat?" He asked his dog while scratching its ears.

"It's late. I better get going. Have a great day." I excused myself. "And you too." As, James said this, Kimble barks too, as it is also saying goodbye to me.

I clandestinely unlocked the oak main door, enter the bungalow and carefully walk through the wood-floor of the hallway. But, just not my luck, I make a crack sound. I hate this wood floor! Why in all the floors, the only hallway's floor is made up of wood?

"I heard you." "I know." I lift both my hands, singing surrender.

"Who give you consent to come home after 9?" Dad asked in irritation. "What? Dad, I am 19!" "18, precisely. You haven't had your birthday this year." I just nod angrily. Yeah, right!

"I am tired. Let me sleep." With those words, I climb up the stairs.

"Okay. No dinner for you. No supper, nothing. And we need to talk." I moaned while looking upward. "Dad, I am tired."

"About Professor Ken, what's that all about? Quitting from '360'? Are you out of your mind?"

"Dad, we talked about it hundreds of time. I am a cheerleader, dad. And of course I'll never be good in ice hockey, Tae Kwan do, Greece, and everything! Except if you asked me about what make up that I wore, the latest fashion, about how to design a dress…"

Dad puts his hand in the pocket, glaring at me with sharp wrinkled eyes.

"Go to your room now," and with that, he walks away.

I shake my head slightly and make my way upstairs. "Stop eavesdropping!" I snap Steven's head when I saw him at the end of the banister.

"Ouch!"

"Now go to your room. Go! Go!" I push him hard towards his bedroom which just across of mine. I slam the oak door, and sigh heavily while leaning against it.

CHAPTER III

"Mrs. North, get into the rink, now!" Mr. Dabore ordered while pointing towards the rink. What the heck—my eyes could not stop blinking. What am I going to do?

I look down at my cyan skates. "Grab the hockey stick. Will you please hurry up, Mrs. North?"

I exhale deeply before grabbing my hockey stick and skates into the rink. "Recount the steps and techniques that I had taught you for the past few weeks, will you?" I bite my bottom lip.

Sheesh! My legs are trembling. I had never been put in a game, even though in a practice time! The girls are laughing at me while I made my way into the icy rink. I tightened my grip on the hockey stick. I had never adored ice hockey!

"You better watch your butt, newbie." The captain of my team, Helecka Folmes, one of 360, warned me. But, she enjoyed ditching every meeting that 360 handled. "Alright, hook up! Take Yvaine's position." Helecka ordered around.

Yvaine's eyes wide open upon hearing the order. "Wait! I wanna play! Nobody's going to take what is mine."

"What 'was' yours. She needs to become the right wing. Move it, Yvaine." Yvaine throws away her hockey stick, a sign of protesting. Mr. Dabore is aware of her manner and that made him mad. "If you want to be a good player, you should respect your equipment! Pick it up now!" he taught her. Mr. Dabore always taught us to respect our equipments.

Yvaine squats and takes the stick lazily before skating out of the rink. I sigh. What a tense! When I was about to take my position, the whistle blows already! What the—

"Hey, I am not ready y—." I grunt.

That's hurt a lot! But, the other players ignore me. I try to stand up, but Kelly, from the opposite team pushes me, making me stumble back on the ice. I clench my teeth.

And…there the puck goes. Into the goal! My team lost. Helecka skates directly towards me, with rage. "Don't be too slow to stand up, will ya?"

With that, she skates back to her position, the centre. I groan. This is harder than I thought.

I did see that Stefanie, who is in the right defense position always fall, but, I don't know how she manage to stand up that haste and resumes the game like nothing happen. As for me, along the game, I had always being push and fall, push and fall. There is once when

I get the puck at my stick, I try my best to control it but I am suck! I only being able to protect the puck for only 5 seconds before someone shove me and make me fall down—again.

The game ended at last. When I was about to make my way to the gym locker, I saw Yvaine perceiving the rink at one of the concrete bleachers. When I smile at her, she ogles at me. I puff before continue my way to the gym locker. It's just a game. What a big deal about it?

I am at my limit, exhausted. I walk out of my locker and trot lazily along the hallway to the exit when someone admonished me from behind. It's Zen. He looks like just taking his shower.

"Where are you from?" I asked him curiously. He points toward the back door.

"Stable. I just finish my horse-riding activity and done my shower."

"Going home now?" "No. Still have something to catch up."

I was astounded. "It almost night and you still have class to go?" Zen chuckled upon seeing my amaze reaction.

"No. But, I have something that I need to settle before walking contently to home," he replied. Speechless, I left him and make my own way.

I glance back, and saw Zen walks the other direction. That did arouse my curiosity. I follow him down the dark alley behind the university.

He keeps walking and walking and I don't know it lead to where. Trotting lazily, I don't think he is thinking about going home yet. Suddenly, I halt. I must get home before dad nagging me about it. But…I really want to know what Zen is up to.

I look at the front, and…I saw nothing. I sigh. Yeah, I should go home now.

"AAAHHH!!!"

That really astounded me! Zen appears out of nowhere and now he is standing in front of me

. "I knew it. I had six senses. Watcha doin'?" he asked with that dumb smile on his face.

I groan. "I thought about following you, but it almost night so I make up my mind."

Zen inhales deeply while considering something. "It's rude to spy on me, especially when I am one of the 360." I roll my eyes. What excuse is that?

"By the way, where are you going?" "Anywhere I want for sure." That answer pissed me off.

"Come on! Send me home!" Zen gapes upon hearing my pleading. "Woo! You follow me here yet you expect me to send you back? That's funny because I am not going anywhere. I am staying here."

"What? Just go home or your dad might scold you." I told him, which somehow had made Zen lets out a big sinister laugh.

He pats my shoulder. "I am not a baby, Stellar North." I pout.

He really pissed me off. Or maybe he was right. Maybe I am the baby one here. Still coming home before night even I am 18 already. 19!

"I am going with you." "Girls aren't allowed." "I am a woman." With that, Zen gives me up and down look at every inch of my body.

"Maybe I am short. But, I am still a woman." I added when I found out that I had difficulty to look straight into his eyes because he is too tall and I had to look up to speak to him. He shrugs before continue walking.

After a while, we arrive at... unknown place for me, and familiar place for him. "Welcome to our secret grotto." Zen said, opening his arms widely.

"A grotto? It doesn't seem like one." I said. Zen scoffs. "Whatever."

Behind the grotto, I heard people shouting and cheering indistinctively. I take a glance outside and saw a group of guys playing basketball. When I enter the 'grotto' back, I saw Zen already changes his shirt into a sleeveless gray shirt.

"Are you going to play?" I asked him in surprise.
Zen just smiles before running into the basketball court.

He is prowess in it. I just watch. The night wind is chilling indeed. But, the guys are all sweating. Then, I saw something that really attracts my attention!
It's James, the beach guy! He is in there, playing with Zen and other fellows. I walk into the basketball court and seat at one of the wooden bleacher.

"Hey, check it out! It's a gal there!" The other guys start whistling and glancing at me. All I did was ignoring. That's what my dad taught me to do.

"Don't bother her. She is with me." Zen shouted from the court while playing. Yeah, right! Then I saw James smiling at me and I realized that I did the same thing too.

"I am Mike. Mike Janider." I shake hand with Mike who just come and seat beside me. He's an African but he got this sweet kind face.

"I am Stellar. Stellar North" "Hey, Janitor is putting on the bait!" a shirtless guy shouted. Mike just grins, maybe already used to that teasing.

"They called you Janitor?" Mike nods jubilantly, answering my question. "Is it because of your names almost sound likes it?" again, I asked him. He then made a click sound. "You said it."

I gape. "I was just asking if it is true. I am not judging your name." Mike laughs out loud.

"It's okay. Seriously it's okay." He calmed me.
"Is Zen going to play all night long?" I asked. "Maybe, like the other nights. Anyway, he's good in it. Without him, we'll lose. He is like—the hope of basketball team. That's why '360' chose him." Mike said. I can't let my eyes stop from looking at Zen. He is just—too good. I remember the game that I had this evening, the ice hockey.

And the Greece lesson, and Tae Kwan Do, and everything else that I must be good at, I'll never make it! I hate it! I put my hands at my face. I don't want to face the truth that I am never good at anything. Mike saw it and tilted his head, asking why.

"I will never be good at what I'm supposed to be." I confessed.
"360? Well, everyone had hard time in it." Mike said.

"But, they did it! They passed the test; they are like the great champion! Unlike me, I hadn't been good at anything since I join this—this whole thing!"

"You can try harder." That voice is from behind, James. I groan. He'll never understand. "You don't know! You'll never know what it feels like." Mike frowns upon hearing my word.

"Don't say that to the only great guy with sea." I look at Mike, and then look at James. "What do you mean 'the guy that great with sea'?"

James spanks Mike. "I told you no!" He scolded the African man.

"James Billiard, the only '360' guy who get to be prowess with sea, river and everything that has to do with water! The last water bender!" Mike exaggerated.

I frown. "That's not funny!" I told him.
James smirks. "It is funny. They keep calling me 'the last water bender'. I kind of like that name." he said while laughing. "No! I mean the '360' thing. It's not funny, okay?!"

"And why is that?" Zen appears behind me, asking the clarion question.
"I—I don't understand. Is James is one of our university student?" Zen wipes his sweat with a small yellow towel before made his way towards the bleachers.
"'360' is not only in our school. There are a lot of them." Zen explained.

That news—shocked me in every angle! So, there's still a lot of '360' out there! "Why did I didn't know about it?" "You always come late in every meeting."

I sigh. "So, there must be a base, a centre to all of this, right?" I asked excitedly.

James gulps the water from bottle while looking at me. "What are you trying to say?" Mike asked with a big frown. "I say that let's go to the base!" I shouted.

James accidentally spurts out the water and cough.

"What? It's a great idea, right guys? Guys?"
"No, it's not." James said. "You should not go there too." Mike agreed to James.

"Why?" "We afraid that you can't—get along with the true situation…" Zen said.

"Like…" I try to make them continue what they are trying to say because I am eager to know the truth. "Like what?" I shouted impatiently.
"Nothing. It's been a long night, isn't it?" Zen asked James. "Hey, don't avert me!" Right, they are trying to run away!

Whatever it is, I'll try to get to the base, because I want to know something. Why had I been chosen to be in this group? What's the truth that I had to adapt with? What is this entire thing about? So many questions make me eager to go!

CHAPTER IV

"Stellar North! What is this?!"

I clicked my tongue. "Are you trying to fool around with me?" Professor Anora keeps nagging. Well…I didn't manage to complete my Greece homework of course. I had been visiting Zen's place all night, and talk to Mike nonstop. He sure is funny.

Getting back from classes, I am already tired when I heard cheers from somewhere nearby. Not to mention that I am so grateful to meet my high school friends waiting for me in front of the university.

"Hi!" a black wavy hair girl greeted. "We missed you so much, Stellar. Look at you, and your hair! You're styling a lot!" Another red hair girl hugs me. I put my hands on Krista's and Evaline's shoulders.

They are my best buddies in the whole world. Krista is running a restaurant with her family and she's currently doing culinary art. Evaline? She's also a bright kid. She is thinking about taking statistics. She likes Math, a lot! We got into Krista's car, a black elegant Volkswagen and drives through the city, laughing and singing happily. Weird.

It's like I totally forget about my problems at my place. "So, tell me, what had you done in the university." Upon hearing that question from Krista, I moan.

"Stop talking about academic and school with me. I'm bored already."

"What?" Evaline, who is wearing big black glasses, pulls it up to her gold hair while staring at me. "You'd never being bored talking about academics and stuffs, nerdy." She said. Her blue eyes glitter even more.

"It's not like that. The thing is…I had been packed in a group of people that was smart ass and… I got the lowest marks in everything that I do with them." Hearing my confession, both my buddies gape.

"No way!" They said simultaneously. I nod at them, emphasizing what I had said.

"Our genius Stellar is being the lowest in class in a new place." Hearing the 'word' genius coming out from Krista's mouth is making me a bit sad. "What's wrong, honey?" Realizing the mood changed in me, Evaline asked.

"Well, I am no longer the perfect, genius, popular and pretty Stellar that the high schooler used to see me back then. I had become the nothing girl."

Evaline pats my head and my back, somehow trying to comfort me. "I'll guarantee everything will turn out to be better." "Me too." "And where are we going?"

"We're going to…"

"…Pajamas party!!!"

With that, the three of us rock and roll inside the car.

***

I can smell high school energy around Krista's mansion. We never get bored to attend pajamas party in here. Well… The thing is our pajamas party is not only a party…but also a havoc party. It's the time where we will release all our tension with academics and lives.

And tonight, we're going to do it again despite of our age!

"Hannah, catch!"

"Oh, careful Stellar! You're going to break this cup!"

"Only if you don't manage to catch it,"

And here we are, giggling and chuckling and dancing and gossiping about guys in Krista's massive bedroom, decorated blue. She always love that color.

"Alright! Time to get serious, ladies!" Krista shouted while standing on the queen size bed.

We all clap our hand, just like when we are watching One Direction doing live concert in front of us. "Okay, no more stress, no more problems! All we do now is gossiping…" Evaline added.

Well…we are the high school cheerleader team. Me, Evaline, Krista, Hannah, Stacey, Kelly, Julia, Maria, Blaire and Andrea miss the time when we spend time together. We can loco sometimes, but they always there when one of us is in problem.

"I was thinking that I want to complain about my new life in the community college." Andrea, who's inheriting Chinese facial from her father, said while bouncing on the bed.

"No! We promised to not talking about that since we're here, got it?" Krista protested. "But, I really need to talk about it."

"No. You'll ruin the mood." Blaire scowled.

"Yeah, we're here to forget. And tomorrow, we'll remember back." Julia added while gulping some juice from the table across the bed.

"But, if you insist, we can listen, can't we?" I asked. Well, I also want to share my problem with them too.

"If you say so, Stellar." Andrea sighs. "I want to become the cheerleader in my college. But, they all are so fat and—lazy to jump, move around and do scary stuff, like being thrown up in the air!"
Other girls show a frustrating face. I moan loudly.

"I thought you are going to tell us the biggest problem of the biggest problem!" mad, I throw her the big fat pillow from under my thigh.

"It is the biggest problem. I mean, how can I work with them if they being lazy ass?" I look down. Not wanting to hear anymore.

"It's better than me, Andrea." I told her.

"And what's with you?" she asked me.

Everyone starts to gather around me, making a circle whereas I am in the centre.

"You've got to believe this. Stellar is no longer the smartest in her class!" Whith Krista telling them this, all the ladies gasp.

"So, no one's respecting you now?" Stacey asked eagerly.

"No. I feel like a loser. I mean—this whole time I was respected. Then, I was dump. And they make me play extreme sports, like ice hockey!"

I express my feeling to them.

"Ice hockey?" Julia, Hannah and Blaire start to giggle and it turn out to be a big laugh.

"We feel sorry for you, but no worry because there are still more hot chicks in your campus!" Maria and Blaire show a cross sign before dancing happily with the rhythm of a rock song.

I touch my forehead! It's no use talking to them. They don't have brains after all.

"Talking about hot chick, what's happen to that hot but not hot, cold but not cold guy?" Stacie asked. She is talking without looking at us, still locking herself at her phone.

"Well…I haven't seen him in ages." I said.

"Come one, he's your cousin. How can you not see him when you always visit him every fortnight?" Kelly asked with disbelief. Kelly and Stacey look at each other. "You're right. I should visit him too. It's been a long time." I nod slightly.

CHAPTER V

"Hi, Aunt Ressa." I hug her tightly. She is my dearest aunt in the world. I don't know why but I had this creepy feeling that she is exactly like my mom. She got 3 kids, Troy, Tristan and Tiffany. I decided to have a stay over at their house this weekend because Aunt Ressa is having a huge birthday party for her second son, Tristan. He is the same age as me. And his birthday is exactly as mine, so we are considered as twin-not-twin.

That idea is kind of fun, but Tristan is unlike my other two cousins, he is really a cold-blooded person. I envy him a lot. Why? I have my reasons.

He is like a big cold, quiet old brother to me, although we're in the same age.

When we're little, we always play puzzles and riddles together. Actually, I am the one who always cling on him so that I can get to play with him. But, he keeps averting me… making me want to cling on him even more. But, I never got to solve one riddles before he does.

I also envy of his short wavy brunette hair, with chilly red eyes and he got a pale skin too. I wonder why he is the only one in his family with brunette hair—not to mention his eyes, while everyone in his family has black dark hair. I suppose he inherits it from his dad's side.

"Hi, Tristan!" I wave at him, and as usual, he gives no respond at all. That does not offend me at all. He is wearing a crimson sweatshirt with black tracksuits. After opening the main door, he continues his activity; sitting on the posh red sofa while watching a cartoon movie—eating popcorn. Surely he is setting his own cinema in the living room.

"Honey, that's not how you greet your guest! Welcome home, my dear~" Aunt Ressa hugs me so tight that I can't breathe.

"It's nice to see you, Stellar."
Troy greeted. "And you too." I curtsy him while making my way upstairs. This is my second home and I like coming here. Aunt Ressa had built another room for me, because I like to stay here somehow. Steven is going to sleep with Troy whenever we pay our visit at their house. Somehow, it had become a common thing to do; visiting their house once in a fortnight.

"We are going to prepare dinner. What do you wanna eat for dinner?" Aunt Ressa asked with delight.

"I am fine with everything. Don't burden yourself too much." I said to aunt Ressa who is standing at the doorway of my room. "Like you never did that before." Aunt Ressa chuckles while closing the door so that I can have my own privacy.

For once, I take a deep breath. I look outside the big arch window and saw my dad's car pulls over, out on the road and out of my sight. He gonna picks me and Steven up again on Sunday night.

I heard crack sound outside; the sound that been heard when someone walks onto the wooden floor. Well, this house is a bit antique but it is very lavish and exquisite. That's when I heard the bedroom's door in front of my room sways open. It's Tristan. I decided to visit him in his room.

"May I come in?" I knocked on the door but nobody answered. So, I just barge in. I saw Tristan is typing something on the computer. "Who told you to come in?" He asked without even looking at me. "Well—silence means agree." I give him a cranky smile even though he can't see it.

"I have a lot of work to do in here. So, it is better if you just go out for a moment." He answered me without even looking.

I shrug. "No worry. I won't bother you." I look around his room. He decorates it in a really unique way. On the left side of his room, there are music instruments. There's guitar, flute and keyboard. Sticking on the wall are the music notes, which he sticks them on the wall to memorize them. On the ceiling, he had been filling them with constellations, each with name. No wonder he becomes so bright. But, I don't see any books around.

"You're bright!" I suddenly praised him, sincerely from my heart.

"If only I never learn about anything big… I just had to learn what necessary for me." He muttered, or—is he talking to me just now?

"Had you done perceiving?" Suddenly, he asked me. I nod. "Then, get out." Okay, that's harsh. But, I'll be fine, as long as he talks to me. I had always wanted to be his best buddy, best chum, as he is my peer in blood relation. But, he seems like an aloof guy.

We are having our marshmallows at the lawn. Steven is talking non-stop with Troy and Tiffany. Tiffany likes to cling to Steven whenever he is around. Tristan is listening to the headphone, doesn't has any interest to make friend with me. I am having my fun time, talking to Aunt Ressa. She is really kind.

"Tristan, will you come and make friend with your guest?" Aunt Ressa asked in irritation, uncomfortable with her son's manner. Tristan rolls his eyes and walks into the backyard door, and into the house. Aunt Ressa forced a smile.

"I never know whose manner he is inheriting." I giggle at her words. "Maybe it's from Uncle Wyatt."

It's 3 a.m. I really want to pee. Really need the ladies right now. I reach for my bunny slippers and straightening my pajamas before walking out of the bedroom. My hair is really straggling around, such a mess when I look into the mirror.

I was yawning and stretching when I heard clanging sound comes from Tristan's room. I made some eavesdrops as I was curious. Then, it becomes silent. Slowly, I turn the knob around and sneak into his dark room. It is so dark that I only see with the help of the moonlight. When I look on the queen size bed—

Tristan is gone! He is no longer on his bed. I observe everything when I realize that I feel chilling air sip into my spine. I turn around, and saw the curtains swaying. The window panes are half closed and I saw shadows behind the bushes. What the—

I quickly grab my grey hooded sweater, put on my tracksuit, bring torchlight with me, hand phone (vital) and shove my shoes before running in haste, following the tract left by Tristan. Where is he going in the middle of night? Not night, its morning already, early in the morning. I manage to catch him. He is in perfect sport attire, drenched with sweat already. Exercising?

We had been walking since then. I was so tired but I could not stop. Curious had won me!

At last…we arrived…to the place…where I always longing for…

CHAPTER VI

I could not move since then, my legs were tucked to the mud ground. I was astonished! I see Tristan climbs down the hill, into the large cleave. What inside it had astounded me! I recognized this place. It is—the base of 360!!!

THE BASE OF 360, THE CENTRE OF ALL ACTIVITIES

It is really chilly that I tighten the sweater around me. I was in between the crowd. They are chatting, drinking hot coffees. Some of them are playing with swords at the place provided. They also had a stadium. I can hear cheering and shouting from inside it. I can see a really huge infirmary at the edge of this whole place. In the centre of the base, there was a really beautiful posh and huge sky-cracker building. The building is full of lights and moving things attached to the wall, going up and down (I don't know what it is, mini robots maybe).

There's a lot of square on the ground, maybe a pathway to somewhere else. Suddenly, one of the square slides open, revealing a huge big hole. I don't think it's a hole when a few people come from under it.

I had a quick look around. I feel like I am in another different world where I can't describe by word. This is amazing! How do I know that this is the base of the 360? It is because at the very top of the sky-cracker building, there are three emeralds circulating the top; they are like generating energy to the building which had gave power to what surround it.

This is weird. Why on Earth would Tristan comes here? And I don't know that it takes only by walking from my aunt's house to reach here. I should have known about it!

"Hey, you're newbie?" I turn around and saw a brutal-looking woman with black—uniform, perceiving me from head to toe.

"Uh—I'm 360, too." I said to her but the woman groans. She called upon a man, seems a bit old. "Check her. Make sure you don't miss out something." She ordered the man. I could not see his face clearly because his face is covered by the shadow of the cap.

"There's nothing, Ma'am Phella." The man said. The woman, called Phella shoves me, pushing me to an isolated tent. After entering the tent, she pushed me hardly on the ground, making me stumble and grunted.

"Who are you? You have no right to this authority." She said to me, more to yelling actually. I sigh. "I am truly one of 360. If not, ask anybody at my university." I confronted her.

"That's the problem. We don't list you by college or university. We list you by number, trespasser." She started to talk.

Suddenly, the alarm building starts to ring. It made a really irritating loud sound. Phella rolls her eyes. "He got to be kidding me. Alright, turn that off now Alex. You gonna wake all the students in this area." She talked towards the 'walkie talkie'. That's when a man barges into our tent—with gun on the stout hands.

The man frowns when he saw me. "Who is she, Olivia?" the man in black suit asked. Olivia Phella shrugs without looking at me. "She said she is one of us, though it's really dubious."

The man comes closer towards me. He lifts up my chin by using the end of his M16A2. I cannot stop gulping, this is serious. I should not come here in the first place if I am not invited!

"Tell me the truth! Are you the deceiver?" he asked, this time in a higher tone.

I gape. "Deceiver? I know nothing about deceiver!" The man glances at Olivia, then at me again. "What's wrong, Alex? Counter some problem there?" she asked him. Alex just remains silence. He grabs my arms and forces me to walk out of the tent.

It hurt my stomach a lot when I step my foot outside. A troop of army had surrounded the tent where I had been pushed into. Am I looking like a brutal criminal to them?

I know where we are heading, to the centre of the area, into the tall building. Along the way, I can hear Alex and Olivia are disputing about something, but I don't know what it is because I can't hear them clearly.

"I had tagged all 360 students, with numbers. Patricia is the last that was labeled which was 3 weeks ago! If she is one of us, we could have known because she will be registered by her institute, which I had gave her the labeled as well as the other." He explained his concern.

Then, he lets go of my hand and try to 'take off' my cloth! "Hey!" I try to stop him from doing that, but he is so strong that I can't resist.

Well, misunderstanding actually. He is not trying to take off my cloth, but he is revealing the part of my stomach.

"See, she is not labeled!" he shouted with his eyebrows rise. I bit my bottom lip.

"I am being registered! My professor told me so, and I saw my name in every list of '360' in my institution!" I defend myself. I am not an intruder!

"Stellar?" Okay, that voice can be my life saver and it seems familiar. We all look around to seek for the voice. But, I feel a really big relief when I saw Zen running towards us.

"Morning, sire." Zen greeted the rude man.
"Morning, 45."
"I heard you got a victim." He said to Alex. "Well, this girl claimed that she is one of us, and it seems that you are familiar to her, 45." Alex explained the situation.

I roll my eyes. Why Alex keeps calling him number? He has name, his name is Zen O'Conner!

"She is one of us indeed." Zen protected me.

"Then, explain to me why is she not being registered here, and labeled?" Zen grimacing and I know he doesn't has the answer to that question. I mean it is so suddenly. The best way to know is to ask the professor at my school!

That's when something that always annoyed me appeared, Tristan Mc'Ashton.

"What are you doing here? Are you spying on me?" That clarion question from my cousin annoyed me. I am his cousin! I have a right to know where he wants to go in the early morning.

"2, it's a good day, isn't it?" Olivia smiles bashfully toward Tristan.

"Not when I found my cousin is here with us." Tristan replied. "Hey, I am one of you. And you never told me you are also one of 360." I argued. "None of your business!"

"Alright, cousins. Cut that out!"

Tristan glared at me before heading toward somewhere else. I want to follow him but Alex fettered my movement. Zen scoffed.

"Come on. She is not that dangerous lassie. Look at her, such a puny body can't harm you." Zen said.

"It seems that you forgot our method of learning here, 45. Annihilation sometimes doesn't come from your physical strength, but from that small brain!" With that last words from Alex, Zen could not help but only stand there, perceiving me being dragged into the building.

I should come earlier to class! I should know the maze of this building! I should pay attention when Prof. Ken told me to do so, because now, I was stuck in the middle of a small room which can only fit 5 persons in here. Everything in here was white; the ceiling, the mosaic tiles, the door…the fan, the light, the chairs, the desk. I don't know whether the dawn had arrived, or the sun had rose or anything about the time, plus my hand phone had been snatched away.

Olivia comes in, bringing a laptop with her. Alex is behind her, with another freckled old man, wearing white lab coat. "Good morning."

The old man clears his throat before starting his conversation.

"So, you claim that you belong to us, which mean you should be prowess at something. Show us then, what languages do you speak?" that question from Olivia makes me roll my eyes.

So, I must take an exam to prove that I am who I am! "I am not that good in languages. Hey, I am still in my practice!" The old man grimaces. "It had been 8 months and you still practicing?" I support my head with my hand, bored of this conversation.

"I am not that fast-learner, okay? So, I need more time than any other else did."

Alex gives me his cold gaze. "That is something that really annoyed me! How come a girl with a moderate brain was chosen to become a part of our organization when we said that we wanted students with high IQ?" he suddenly yelled at me while banging his hand on the desk.

"I don't know! Besides, I never walk in for the test to be in part of it. Professor just chose me, and I try to quit, but he won't let me."
"Good excuses, talking like you are the most important person who contributes the most in our group." He argued back.
"I did not mean that!" I am really mad and in rage right now! How dare this old guy accuse me like I am too obsessed with being one of them?

"Guys, break off. I found her profile." Olivia decreased the tense.

"What? You stalked me?"

Olivia ignores me and keeps looking at her laptop. "Not so much information about her. You don't fill out the requirement form, aren't you?"

"Like I said, I never walk in for the test and I don't fill any forms. I think that's a major reason of why my name is not in the list?" I shrug.

Suddenly, Alex and the professor seem to be interested with the laptop. Did my profile really astound them? "So, you are Stellar North." Alex murmured. "Of course I am Stellar North."

"If you got into this base, it's mean you are ready to be train like what you have to. You know that, right?" I just shrug, not getting what he meant by it.

When they are walking out of the room, I heard Alex whispers something to Olivia. He said that before I leave, they should give me 'that' thing. I narrowed my eyes because I want to focus more on 'that' thing. But, I just don't know. The old man just nod before they shut the door closed.

In a minute, white gas filled the room. Oh my—what's happening? I go to the door and bang at it. "Someone just open this door!" I try to turn the knob but it doesn't seem to work. I am deadly panic and frenetic. So, they are trying to kill me eh? Not that easy!

I squat on the floor, touching every single tile, pushed it slowly. This is going to take ages! When I found nothing, I go to the wall. The smoke is filling almost the whole room as the room is so small. When I lost all my hopes, I suddenly found something on the ceiling, just exactly beside the fan!

There's a tiny line that form a circle! It is so tiny but because my vision get more narrow, I had being able to see it. I put chair on top of the other chair to reach the ceiling. But, it was such a failure! So, I drag the desk and put it exactly under the circle line, putting all the chairs on it and start climbing the desk. Please let me reach it-- When I was about to push the ceiling, I cough and that makes me fall down. Everything falls down. It is so frustrating! My vision gets really weak and vague. I try to climb it once again, but I start to wobble because I had lost some of my focus due to the heavy smoke. Then, for the last time, I push the ceiling again—

CHAPTER VII

My head, it's swirling. I feel like someone had just knocked them so hard that I can't lift them up. I try to open my eyes, but the vivid light that penetrates them is so painful that it made me hard to see. So, I just keep them closed back.

Then, I heard familiar voice chatting on my head. A girl's voice…I try to recall the voice, but every time I did that, I ended up hurting my brain even more. "Good day, Stellar. Now, open your eyes, your lazy ass." I frown. If only she knows how pain it is right now.

"Rise and shine. You had get a good sleep weren't you?" I try to open my eyes to see the owner of that voice. No matter how pain it is, I don't want to keep them shut forever.

I knew that I knew the voice! It's Helecka, my ice hockey captain! I can recognize by the sound of her lewd voice. "She's up, Olivia. I told ya! My voice is always the best alarm."

"Hmmm—Thanks, 95." Olivia said in gratitude.

"Anytime!" Helecka helps me to sit straight. I feel like I am on a ward bed. I don't like the smell of the infirmary at all.

"95, you can continue practicing hockey. I believe you need them after you hurt your calf last game, right?" Helecka gives her a lopsided smile.

"Well, Olivia. I don't think I need 'em right now. I am heading to my college. Want something on the way?" when Helecka asked her that question, Olivia taps her chin slowly.

"How about some ice-cream?" "You got me!" With that, Helecka rushes out of the infirmary.

I watch Olivia does her job, moving up and forth, putting all the medicines back into their shelves, washes her hand and gets ready to leave the infirmary.

"What am I doing here?" I asked her. But, she seems like in rush and I believe she will not answer my question right away. Before she leaves, she reminds me with one word. "Stay." Then, the white glass door shuts close.

I can't just stay, must I? I get off from the ward bed. When I try to walk, I am wobbling. It's get pretty dizzy some times. I see that everything around me becomes four. I grip on something, avoiding myself from falling. I grab the roller tray, and made them roll until I reach the glass door. I try to push it but—its lock. Why give me warning if you intend to lock me in here? I sigh, leaning my head against the door while closing my eyes.

I gulp once more, "Please open this door. I wanna go home..." I said, half whispering. That's when something astounded me. The door seems to be unlocking by itself. I know that right now, my eyes are wide upon with amazement Weird. I look left and right. There's no one in the main hallway. I follow the exit sign until I find my way out, through the backdoor. This building is pretty huge.

A step before the exit door, there's a full-length mirror which I just happened to realize when I try to turn the knob. I look at myself in it. What a mess. I rub my black hair. They are like had been shocked with electrics so I comb them with my fingers a bit. Then, I realized that I am not wearing pajamas anymore. No hooded sweater, no tracksuit...not my cloth. In fact, I am wearing a green patient cloth! "I hate it!" I shrieked. I turn around; try to see which side does look good on me. I pout. Nothing did look good on me if I continue wearing this absurd uniform. I grimace, 'Feel like a hogwash prisoner,' I mused. Enough of it, Stellar!

I step out of the exit door and a very bright ray of sunlight makes me stumble back. I yanked and crawled back into the building while shutting the exit door with my leg. "What was that?" I asked myself. Since when did I become too fragile toward sunlight? My head spinning even more. Okay, this is definitely not good!

"Didn't she tell you not to escape?" I just take a glance to see the speaker. It's James.

"What are you doing here?" I asked him, which actually I have no interest in whatsoever he's doing here.

"I just finished my business with Mr. Lickenson. Wow! You look—haggard and horrible." "Thanks. I take that as a compliment." I wipe my nose, feeling like something just come out from it.

"Did they drug you?" I shrug because I don't want to know.

I don't give a hell about it anyway. He squats, try to take a best view of my face. When he tries to touch my cheeks, I snap away his hand. I don't like something on my face! James sighs with remorse and resentment.

"They did give you something." James said, looking confident with his conclusion.

"I don't care a hell, okay? In fact, I don't care at all! They wanna use my body, they wanna experiment me, they wanna crush me from inside and hit my damn brain, I don't care! Now, get me out of this *shithole*!" I don't know why James groans loudly, and with regret when I said what I feel now.

"That is a no go way! Not until you stop cursing!" I keep my mouth shut for a while when he said that I am cursing.

"I did not cursing! You are the one who did, jab!" James bites his bottom lip before carrying me on his arms. I was so shocked and start to waggle around. I jabber something that I don't even understand as all I want is for him to put me down.

I let out a heavy growl when he drops me on a big couch situated in an affluence office, with glass furniture.

"What did you do to her, Mr. Lickenson?" I heard James' yelling. I look up, but my vision become vague that I lie down again. I was so exhausted to stand up. "What do you mean, '34'?"

"My name is James and they are not numbered, okay?! Now, tell me. What did you gave to her? What drug? She keeps cursing and I don't like it! It is such a repugnant manner!" Mr. Lickenson chuckled.

"Neither do I. But, we have to, for our own sake." "What sake?"

"Gosh! You all are too nuisance! I need my sleep!" I screamed in the room which produced loud echo. The silent had made me feel really relish and I realized that I smile while recovering my sleep. Not until someone grips my hand stoutly. "Ouch!" I yanked.

"You still have time to sleep right now? Are you insane?" My ears are pricking because James' voice was so loud.

"There's no use to yell at her. She doesn't care at all. She'll be safe as long as the drug is effective." Mr. Lickenson said. Now I can see a clear vision of Mr. Lickenson. Ughh…It is Alex. Alex Lickenson.

"I am not affected by the drug, Lichen… It's just—I am exhausted. Now, let me sleep until I gain my energy." I babble. Suddenly, it turn pitch black.

CHAPTER VIII

"I am apprehension about her, but guessed I am wrong." A cute guy's voice said. "Duh. Neither do I. Who thought her to be that puny—and benign?" Another girl's voice can be heard.

"Don't sound so sweet and soft spoken. You are derisive and it cannot be altered." The guy with the cute voice replied.

"Ugh~~ Whatever, Simon." The girl besides him said. "She disheartened me. She seems slow and—..." "...Stupid?" Simon continues the word that the girl is about to say. "You all exasperated me. Why don't you all get out for a while?" A stern lady's voice appeared.

I feel someone sits on the bunk beside me, but I just don't want to open my eyes yet. "Sorry. That conversation is inadvertent and they are still small to judge something." The sweet-voice girl inhales deeply before I heard water spatters beside me. At last, I open my eyes. I dodge the white vivid light with my left bare hand.

"Rise and shine."

It's a teen girl. She is so beautiful with icy eyes; it is so blue like seeing a wave of ocean in the shining eyes, with straight white hair, small lips and pale skin. "Ma'am Olivia sent you here so that I can take care of you."

"Oh… Thank you." I said in gratitude. I was tried to get up when she encumbered me.

"I am obliging to help. The drug still not obliterate yet, so you should not move." She said. I get back to my former position. She places the wet small drape sheet on my forehead.

"What is this place?" I asked blankly. "Oh? This is our cabin. We're in Wing B area, cabin number 90 until 179." I gave her a cranky smile as that's not what I mean.

I clear my throat because I feel funny.

"Is something wrong?" she asked with a concern look.

"The drug is too taxing for me." "I knew." "What did they give me?" The teen girl swirls around, gazing at my eyes.

"It's confidential. I should not tell you." "Then, tell me your name." "Wenda Houshborne, but they prefer to call me Gwen." After hearing her name, I asked her another question.

"What is your number? You know—they call people here by number."
"90. But, they don't call 90 people with number; instead they call us by name." This is a fun fact. "90 only?" I raise my eyebrow.

"Students with number 1, 90, 180 and 270, 4 of us are not called by number. We automatically become chief for our troop." She explained explicitly.

I watch her does her job, exactly like what Olivia did back in the infirmary. "When can I leave?" "Unknown." She answered haste.

"I like your hair and your eyes…" I start to put bait. "Don't fawn over me. I may seem small, but I am not."
"Oh…How old are you?" Gwen ignored my question, maybe too tired to answer. "I am assuaging my life here since I don't know when will I get 'discharged'." I said, giggling, as I'm feeling like I had been hospitalized. "Insipid." She answered and left this cabin. I stop blinking. Why her manner is exactly the same as Tristan?

I look down at my thumb underneath the fur blanket. If I continue to become 360, I will definitely besmirch the name of this organization. But, I must be sanguine! At least, they don't kill me here which mean, I am still have chance to be accepted into this group.

I walk out of the cabin slowly. Only to see the most beautiful scene in my entire life! This place is made up of ice, with a lot of cabins around. The cabins are drill and named on each ice door. I smile widely. This is so cool!

I never expected to found kids in here, and adults too. They wear tweeds of colored cloth, and they all have aqua headbands on their head, making them look like a mere ninja.
The alarm bell made a loud noise that piercing my ears. Gwen rushes out of nowhere and hurried toward the edge of the wing. When I perceive the cabins again, everyone had lined out in front of their room, by numbers. I heard some quarrel at the edge which attracts me toward the sound.

"I told you hundred times don't cross the line!" Gwen pushes a Japan guy who had sharp black eyes with a wavy spiking black hair; he also wears headband, but only with black color.

"That's enough, man. Fall back, no more trespassers, okay?" Another guy from his troop consoled him, slowly making him moves backward. Gwen's face was fierce, as she is about to 'eat' that Japan guy. When the Japan guy's leg lifts up from the red cross on the marble ice floor, the siren stops to whirl. They left the wing with rage.

"Nothing happen, get back to your cabins. Remember, lunch at 12. Tick tock." Everybody starts to dismiss except me. Am I in an army camp right now?

CHAPTER IX

I saw a Japan girl seating on the bleachers outside the Wing Building. That Wing Building looks like a gigantic igloo from outside. Really huge, massive and vast! It is also called Wing Building because the upper part of the roof is being divided by two, forming a wing pattern of a bird. No wonder it can occupy 360 students in it. I approach that girl who looks a bit familiar.

"Don't stare at me! It pissed me off!"

"Sorry." I apologized and take a seat beside her when I saw her trying to ignore me. "Hey, I thought you look familiar."

"Whatever, newbie." She answered without even looking.

I pout. I don't like people called me that even though I am not that worth it to become one of this genius groups. I look at the kids that were playing with guns, archeries and swords. Sometimes, I envy them a lot because they are able to do something that is advance than me. I mean, hey—they had been chosen to be in this group since they are so little! That's mean that they are more great than I did.

"YO! Yumiko, I heard your brother is slamming and doing vandalism in Wing A's territory! He is so in rage with Gwen." A guy appeared out of nowhere.

"What's your problem, dude?" "Nothing. Just conveying information." The black guy left. Now I know why she looked familiar.

"What's your name?" I try to create a good atmosphere in here. But, she is trying to insist. Ignoring me, she picks out something from her pocket leather jean. It's look like a code game, with hint to be search and numbers and symbols... Not my type!

At last, she sighs and put the game on her lap. Her smooth black hair drops down from her shoulder when she looks down on the ground. She stares at me with her eyes that look exactly the same as Gwen. "*Atashi Yumiko. Yurishiku onegaishimasu, Setteraru-san.*" After the brief intro, she just walks away. Such a cold girl! Yumiko... Cute name, I wanna call her Ako then!

When I perceive the whole area like a free girl, I heard another whispered quarrel behind a red and black building; seems like a martial arts building because there are so many martial arts' symbols on top of it. "*Demo...*" "*Demo jananaino! *Boku wa...*" It's the Japan siblings. I think they are paired twin. But...I don't think they want it that way.

"What are you doing here? Eavesdrop?" I shook my head frequently when I was busted by Yuki.

"Stellar? Are you following me?" Yumiko appeared behind that beast guy with a somber look. "I am just looking around and I heard you guys are—."

"Don't be so nosy, Stellar!" With that high pitched sound from her brother, I remain silent. By the way, what am I doing here? I suppose to go back home, with or without Tristan. "Yuki, there you are! I'd been looking all over for you! Don't ever skip weekend schedule again! We had a lot of juniors to be trained!" A gangly girl with blond wavy hair rushes toward us.

Now I know that she is in the same wing with Yuki when she wears a black headband too. They all are being labeled by numbers and sub-labeled by headbands color. I touch my head, what am I then?

Ughh- another question with no answer!

"Don't worry about which troop you belong to, you don't need it anyway." Yumiko said. I just realized that she is still here!

"No, I am just curious. It's fun to put on something on forehead like you guys! It's like I am belong to something, and that I am needed." I replied. "The headband doesn't worth you." I grimace, trying to interpret her message just now. The headband doesn't worth me? What's that suppose to mean?

"I am thinking of going home. Do you know which way to exit?" Yumiko halts at my question. She doesn't even turn her back on to look at me. "The way you come here is the way you go home." I start to ponder. The way I come here? I totally forgot about it. My eyes wide open! This is the used of this drug that they just injected in my body this morning! Drug that made me forget.

"Then, show me a way out!"

"I was forbidden to do that."

"Why?" "Because that's the rule: Someone who had been drug cannot be helped." Yumiko said.

The bell at the belfry chimes thrice. Everyone made their way to a particular place, including Yumiko. "Hey, wait up!" I try to catch her up.

The people line up according to their headband color. I interfere in the space between Gwen's troops. I don't wish to meet Tristan by now. They assemble in front of a gigantic glass podium underground. On the stage, there are Alex, Olivia, the scientists and the 4 leaders from each troop. I saw Gwen sitting next to Yuki, with a tight face.

"Where's Stellar? Has anybody seen her?" Alex asked.

Ughh…What did he wanted? I raise my hand which makes everybody turns to me. "What are you doing in there? Are you being allowed to mingle with them?" he asked me through the microphone. "I am?"

Yumiko pushes me forward, making me walk upstage. This is weird, really weird! I can't stop myself playing with the tips of my fingers. Alex really gets me on my nerve.

"Meet Stellar North, the ancestor's—pride." Alex shrugs when he said the word '*pride*'.

Okay, I don't know what he meant by that. The students that assembled in the underground basement start whispering and chattering to each other. I saw Tristan rolls his eyes. I have no idea what's going on. Are they making fool of me?

"She will not be going home until she meets our ancestor's priority. Even if she wants to, she can't, because she forgot her way home. We drugged her! Remember this word! WE DRUG HER. So, if anybody ever wants to take her out of here, you better watch your back. Understood?" Alex said, emphasizing his words.

The students nod simultaneously, like a robot in command. "What am I going to do here? Had I become one of you?" I asked anxiously.

Olivia who is watching since then starts to walk to me until she is so close to me. "No. Beside, you'll never be like us."

I stare at Olivia's eyes as she stares at mine. From behind me, I can hear Alex said the word, "Dismiss," with that, I can hear everyone stepping out from the underground basement. But, I keep staring. What come in my mind is this lady is challenging me! Olivia gives me a lopsided smile before she, Alex and other scientists leave me alone in this cold place.

They think I am not worth it, eh? They think I can't become like them? Maybe, or maybe I am far more genius than them.

"Are you that slow?" The Korean teacher asked. I try to stand up, but I can't, like how I did in my previous Tae Kwan Do training with my dad.

"Stand up!" he shouted again. I am still lying on the mat. I am exhausted, tired and I need food, although I already ate some an hour ago. "Don't sleep on the mat, Stellar!" "I am not sleeping!" I support my weight with both my hands.

I look at Gwen, who has been watching almost my whole training at a distant. My Tae Kwan Do *jogyonim,* Im Dong Ja, gives me a sharp stare, warning me to get up.

Suddenly, the large screen that hangs on the top of the martial art building starts to turn on.

SPONTANEUOS SPARRING FOR 1500 HOURS – 1600 HOURS: 111 VS 112 & 180 VS 45

That is what was written on the screen. With that, everyone starts to arrange a giant mat at the centre of this *dojang*. A *gyosannim* steps on the middle of the mat, calling the participants who are going to spare.

"111 from '*ao*' team and 112 from '*aka*' team, *Charyeot!*" With that, 111 who's wearing blue *hogu* and 112 who's wearing red *hogu* appears from *between* the crowd. Wait—

They are twin? A pair of twin to be exact! Are they going to spare each other? I perceive with amusement. I heard the crowd whispering to one another. "This is going to be fun! It had been months since the twin gets into the ring, eh?" "I bet John hurt a lot after the final match with Joan." I was wondering. Why twin must be put into a fight? It is such an absurd thing. The only thing that will happen is that there will be a large crack between the bonds.

The twin is ready. "*Gyeongnye.*" The twin bows. "*Junbi.*" The twin gets ready with their stances. This is not it! "*Sijak!*"

The crowd starts to cheer, choosing their side. Girls mostly sided John, while guys sided Joan. There they go. From the beginning, Joan starts to attack John with turning kick. That was a good start, but John is so fast that he can see the incoming attack and avoid it. John makes a double kick; it's only a strategy so that he can go more close toward Joan. When he is really near to Joan, he does a chopping. That was quick, making Joan almost falls to the ground.

But, that unawareness of John had made Joan do a front kick and one point for Joan.

The *gyosannim* is about to stop them when John suddenly gets up and do a back kick toward Joan's left cheek. She lets out a heavy groan and stumbles helplessly on the mat. Everyone looks with horror in their eyes. That was—unprecedented by any of us in the room. Contemptuous silent win the match when blood starts to flow from Joan's nose and mouth.

John sighs with deep remorse before carrying up Joan, to the infirmary, maybe. "That was—a damn great match!" Voices start to fill the *dojang* after the twins vanish behind the door. "He never even tries to hurt Joan before, even in the real match!" "That was pretty cool!"

"How can they think something painful as a pretty cool one?!" I start to mumble with rage.

"That's how things go in here." Yumiko whispered to me. "Check out Yuki." She said. "Where?" "There. He's next." She pointed to her brother.

"Who's his rival?" "Team A: Zen." My eyes wide open. There is no way if Zen is going to fight Yuki. It's just—from Yuki's biceps, I knew that Zen is no match for him.

"Don't underestimate Zen. He is no one to be look down at." Gwen said from behind me. Her lopsided smile still can't convince me. "It's their 3rd match this month. Juniors, seniors and even the doctors favor their spare."

With that, Yuki and Zen bow to each other. Yuki's black eyes really penetrate my chest when suddenly, he turned to me. Maybe he is watching his sister who perceives him like they are lovers that just involve in an immense fight.

"Ganbarimasu." Yuki said, even it is half whispering, we can still hear it because his hoarse voice is echoing in the *dojang.* Yumiko bites her bottom lip before leaving the *dojang* without even watch her brother sparring. I want to catch up, but their spare might be interesting and maybe I can learn something from that.

"Stop! We are not going to proceed with the match today!" Everyone lets out a heavy groan, remorse by the announcement from the master of the *dojang.*

"Get back to your training everybody!" "What's wrong, master? We are learning something from thy match!" A lad stood out to give a reason so that the match will still be continued.

"I don't think you are watching the match to ameliorate your knowledge; however, you are watching it for fun and enthusiasm. I believe that 91% of students in here expect them to fight until none of them can get their legs up." Master leaves the room, leaving the students in a disappointment.

"Alright, Stellar! Get back to your position! Wear your *hogu,* now!" Here comes the nosy guy again!

***

"Hey, Gwen…And Tristan." I gave a forced smile toward them when I saw them at the archery field, giggling together.

"Disputing something?" I asked with doubt in my tone. Tristan looks away as Gwen starts to speak. "No. He is showing me something. See. It's a flower, a robot flower. It's so beautiful." Seeing the flower makes me kind of jealous. Why Tristan would make her a flower?

Tristan then gives me a twisted smile.

"Yeah. I was doing something new back then. So, it's kind of fun, to share the fun... I might give them to you as a gift." Gwen's eyes even more shimmering. What is this? A love scene in front of me?

"Why don't you make one for me?" I asked him. "We're cousin, right?" I started to nudge him in hatred.

I notice that he is ogling. "Why don't you play elsewhere?" He shoves me aside, making me walk away from them. "I am not until you make me one." "Don't be a kid, Stellar." With that, Tristan ignores me and keeps talking to someone else! That's made me really mad!

Why on Earth he is not being nice with me?! I HATE HIM.

CHAPTER X

It's pitch night when I get out from the Wing Building. Olivia had let me stay in Gwen's cabin. Gwen is so nice. She lets me wear her pajamas, lends me her toiletries and make sure that I ate sufficient healthy food in here, but, this whole events going so fast that I don't want it to happen to my 'real' life. I feel like I am in a nightmare this whole day which I am unable to wake up.

I decided to run from the camp. One of the major reasons is because of what happened this evening. Ugh- Why must I feel this way? I believe that once I saw the road to where I come from, I can remember my way home. I run to the gigantic wall at the edge of this wrapped place, the wall that had bind and unlock this place from the outer world. Even though this might seem stupid, I must try. I know it is impossible to climb this wall that is far taller than any buildings here. I don't know why such wall must be built high and tall.

"Don't think about it, hogwash." I flinched at the sudden voice coming from behind me. Yuki perceives me from behind with his arms crossed while standing against the martial art building. How long had he been watching me?

"You just have to imagine that you are seeing thing." I told him.

I don't care whether I am not in a great relationship with him so that he can cooperate with me. All I know is that I want to go home, to a safer place where I can meet my dad and Steven. Ughh—I hate the fact that I miss him.

"In your dream, kiddo. This is our region, our place and our rules. So, rules are always rules that meant not to be broken. Go back to your room." Yuki said it while walking closer and closer towards me. It's no use talking to a stubborn head guy like him who never thought of smiling!

I make up my mind, which is to run and hide from him.

"Hey, come back here, you wrench!"

I heard him screaming back there. I am really running like thunder right now. I just don't know where to head but I keep running and running.

While running, someone grabs my legs which had made me fall into a black hole where I can't see a thing. The 'someone' who grabbed me hush me so that I can stay quite.

Not long after it, a light appear from the 'someone's watch. To my surprise, it's Tristan! I embrace him in my arms, feeling really gratitude.

"I knew you were going to do a stupid thing. So, I had awaited for you here." Tristan said, holding his voice.

"Let go of me!" I shake off my arm from him. "Hey, are you crazy?! Just what do you think you're doing back then?"

"Home! I am going home, with or without your help!" Harshly, I snap his hand away.

"Hogwash, listen up. If I help you, I will be in a dead trouble. I don't mind that but so do you." "What do you mean by it?" I asked him.

"I mean that, if I help you, I'm going to be paralyzed and you are going to be deaf and blind." "What do you mean by deaf and blind?"

"Stellar, they can tract you even if you run thousand miles away from them. Once they got you back from your running away action, they'll make you deaf and blind. Many people had experienced it. That's the only way so that you can't tell the base of 360!" "How come you all can get out while I can't?" "Because you haven't vowed yet." "Vow to what?" My mind become even more complex. What is he talking about all of a sudden? What vow?

Tristan sighs.

"You aren't—I mean-. You still don't meet the requirement to make the vow. That's good news for you." Why? I don't understand anything that happens now.
"What I should do now? I just want to go home."

"Yeah, I know you want to but… that way is not where you can go home. That's the way to the deep forest." Tristan shrugs while telling me all of this. I clench his hands.

"Tell me what I supposed to do now." "Stay. Stay until they let you leave." I sigh upon hearing the suggestion. I think I had no choice. At last, Tristan brings me back to my wing room.

Well, it is nice for him to treat me this kind. It's like he cared so much about me. But, when I remember about what had happened this evening, I pout. Maybe he's being gentleman with most of the girls, and I just seeing this side of him a little late.

We are having breakfast in the cafeteria in the wing building. It is such a posh food that being served. I thought we're going to eat what prisoner eats. Gwen pats the vacant seat beside her, wanting me to take a seat there.

After I landed beside her, she whispered something to my ear. "I knew what you did last night." Then, she continued eating like nothing happen. Well, it's kind of awkward atmosphere until Yumiko comes and join us.

"Ohayou" She greeted us. Gwen just nods slightly while I give her a big smile. "So, what's the schedule for today?" the Japan girl asked me. She looks fresh this morning with her hair tied neatly with ponytail style.

"Me? Umm… I'm not certain of it. Maybe…" as I about to say it, Gwen cuts in. "Ice skating. That's what you're going to do today." "Pardon?" I look at Gwen. She can't control my schedule. Olivia never said so! "I never want to do ice skate, especially ice hockey."

"Whatever you say, Helecka will never let you escape. 0830 hours, into the rink." She ordered and lefts me.

I moan deeply. 'INTO THE RINK'. I hate those words so much. I look at Helecka who is preparing the other teammates. Joan is here, she is pretty cool, like a guy. Her short blonde tousle hair suits her fair face really well. She skates into the rink. On the bleachers, I can see John looking at her.

"He is here to aid her. Don't worry about it. He'll only interfere when Joan is injured." Helecka explained to me although I never asked her to. Suddenly, she pushed me into the rink. I stumble on the ice and that's make everybody there laughs. "I don't understand why she can be here. And even being our—." When a teenage girl is about to say something, Joan shuts her mouth with her left hand.

"Say no more." She said before skated to her position. "Back to your place!" Helecka shouted. "Being your what?" I asked again.

There's something that really mysterious here. They are hiding something from me. Something—so deep. What am I? Precisely is…who am I here? Alex said that I am the ancestor's pride. That teen girl from the ice hockey said something about me being theirs. Something weird here.

"Hey, I see that you work hard. Hoho." James comes out of nowhere and admonished me with his cheerful smile same as the smile when I met him for the first time.

I am trotting down the carved pavement, the only park here. This is where I am thinking of going after being hit several times by the ice hockey players. I also like to lean against the lion statue whenever we passed by the archery field in order to go to the Wing Building.

"Yeah…Working hard so that I can escape." "Nah…Don't give me that look. I am sure everything's gonna be fine like it used to be, or even better than that." Well, James always motivates me whenever I feel down. I somehow feel like he is my big brother.

Suddenly, a bell chimes from the top of the main building there. We all look up. What's happening? James grabs my hand as we run to the centre of the base. Everyone does the same. After assembling, we line up according to the numbers. I had being pushed backward for some reason that I don't know. At last, I am at the very back of the line behind Gwen's troop, alone.

Helicopters land not far from the place we lined up. Several men with black coats jump out of it and 'march' toward us. I wonder who they are.

"That guys again! Aren't they tired of disturbing our society?" "Well, they'll never stop until they get one of us." I heard the kids in front of me talking in a really tiny voice, yet I can still hear it.

"Stop chatting about it, kids." The big girl in front of them turns around to warn them. Then, she takes a glimpse at me before looking to the front again. What's that look suppose to mean?

"Where's your chief?" One of the men shouted. I look around to search for Alex and Olivia. Sure they are the chief here, right? Then, Alex, Olivia and the scientists come out from the main building and run toward the coat men. They are exchanging conversation until one of them shouted. "I WANT THE CHIEF!" Everyone starts to grip their fist. Who is the chief to be exact?

CHAPTER XI

Before I know what's going on, I was trembling. Why on Earth—everybody turns to meet my gaze.

I give them a puzzle look. Someone please explain to me what is going on here! Why am I the chief?

They start to push me to the front because I was unable to move an inch. This must be a mistake! During my way to the front, I met Zen's eyes. He just watches me with that somber look. So do James. His face is showing an 'I'm-sorry' look. So did everyone, looking with a deep remorse.

For some time, I arrive at the very front and stand between Olivia and Alex.

"This is the chief that you are waiting for. But, pardon me as she is not well prepared yet." Olivia explained the truth. Seeing my puzzled look, the men in coat frown.

"She looks like an idiot. Are you sure she is the one?" one of the men with thick moustache said.

"Yes. I even carry experiment on her." Alex convinced the man. That men nod simultaneously. Idiot? Who? Me? Ughh...

Suddenly, one of the men brings something out from the chopper. It's small, wrapped in a beautiful cyan knitted handkerchief. Alex frowns out of curiosity.

"What is it?" He asked the man that holding the 'thing'. Without hesitation, he pulls the handkerchief away, revealing a really small device that gives out a small green light on top of it.

The man with beard and grey eyes looks at me, sending me a shiver down my spine. He looks scary. "So tell me, what do you think is it?" I gulp. Why would I know what is it?

"Come on! Tell me, you genius brat!" He shrieked, making me takes a step backward.

With me not making a sound, he sighs. "I am sorry, but she is under a shock as we did so many tests on her. She just needs to be prepared to freshen up her mind so that it'll be working, like it always does." Olivia explained.

"How long will it take to prepare her?" He asked.

"About two weeks? Maybe a month?" Alex answered.

"..."

I could say nothing, but only listen to the adult conversation.

"I'll come back after 2 weeks. Make sure she is well-prepared. Let's get moving." The four guys depart on the gigantic helicopter. The strong wind blows away my silk cyan dress and my hair. So does everyone.

Later, the place is filled with contemptuous silent.

"Dismissed." Alex shouted.

Well, that's horrible! "You all just STOP!" I shrieked. Everyone stops walking and turns to me. "What had happened just now?" I asked frantically. Obviously I am mad because no one tells me anything about everything! Even though I am a girl with only intermediate IQ, they should not treat me like this, like I am some sort of a loco puppy.

Tristan steps out from his line after Olivia nodded to him. He then takes something out of his breast pocket. It's a beautiful crimson pendant.

"This is yours." He gives it to me. I turn the pendant around, seeing my name written on it, 'Stellar North, the light of the future world'.

"It's from our ancestors." Tristan starts to talk.

"It's a shame that she always come late to class. So, she knew nothing about 360's history." Mike said, but someone beside him nudges him, telling him to keep quiet.

"Lee Hanyeol." Olivia called out a Korean guy from the red headband troop, the same as James troop. Hanyeol turns on a hologram which features an old man, wearing a white uniform. I think I had seen him somewhere, like I am familiar to him, but I just don't remember.

"Greetings, my fellow soldiers." The hologram man starts to speak. "If you watch this, that's mean my great grandchild, my pride, my glory, the gospel of '360' organization, is here too." I frown. 'What's that suppose to mean, old man?' I mused. "I am Henry North, the creator of '360' organization where perfectionist is born. After undergoing several experiments and researches, I had found out that the highest limitation of human's IQ will be inherited by my great grandchild, first child of the first child of my second child. If it's a boy, shall name him Steward North. If it's a girl, shall name her Stellar North. That child will inherit the title of The Chief of 360. I'd prepared something for him in order to accomplish my dream which is--" Then, I hear noise which someone had interrupted him. "Enough! Now, get into the car!" With that, the hologram closed immediately.

It's a major mistake! Your theory is absolutely wrong, great grandpapa! Tristan sighs. I tighten my fist, unable to accept what I just heard.

"Henry's second child is William North, and William's first child is your father, Rupert North. You are the first child of him, so he named you Stellar North. By his will, you are the next chief of this secret soldier's organization." Olivia explained.

Now, everything make sense! Why I can't quit from '360', why I can't give up, why father always told me to practice, why Steven keeps pushing me and not to let me quit! My vision gets blurred with my tears.

"It doesn't suit me at all!"

I run out from that area. I run and keep running, into the hole where Tristan had dragged me in last night. I just wanted this all to be a dream. I'm sure will be happy if what great grandpapa said is true, where my IQ reached the limitation of human. But, things are not how it supposed to be now and I can't accept it!

Night falls...

I am still in this dark hole. I am scared to get out of here. Really scared... Suddenly, I hear rustles. Then, it turns quiet again.

"How long will you be sitting in there, punk?" I know exactly whose the voice belong to, Tristan Mc'Ashton, my genius cousin. Why can't I be like him?

"Just get out of there and continue living. Practice so that you can be like what great grandpapa want you to be." I sigh. It's awkward to hear Tristan said something like that to me. If I were the old me, I would be happy to have this conversation with him, but things is not good right now.

"I wanted to be like you. I wanted to be great, genius, intelligent like you." I confess to him. I hug my knees even tighter.

"Alright, I can make you become like me. Just get out of that dumb hole, silly." With that word, I climb up. Then, I can see Tristan and James. I never thought James is with him. There's an unpleasant look in Tristan's facial. Maybe James had forced him to comfort me as Tristan will never say such things to me.

"Why are you all well dressed?" I ask when I saw both Tristan and James are wearing casual outfit but with sport shoes.

"We're going to send you back to my house." My eyes shine with hope. This is the time I had being waiting for. By the day I woke up tomorrow, I'll make sure that everything here is just a dream!

"Don't get your hopes up. Only for tonight! We'll send you back here before dawn." Tristan said while trying to stand up.

"I thought that's the only way to cheer you up, Stellar. After this, can you practice harder than usual for us?" Asking me, James raised his eyebrows. I nod slightly. I can run away after reaching Tristan's home. Or call the police. I am sure that this organization is illegal under government. Olivia even said that this is a secret soldier organization.

Along the way, Tristan just keeps silence while holding my hand.

"Why '360' exist?" I try to talk to him by clinging on him too. I thought Tristan will let my question fades in the horizon, but at last he does answer it.

"To create a perfect world."
"Why want to create a perfect world when we're all now in peace?"
"What do you mean by peace?" Tristan asked me angrily.

"There's no more peace right now. The world is getting near to its end. Violation everywhere, kidnapping, crimes...there's no peace!"

"And what's the point by making '360'? It's only making things worse!" I rebut him. Tristan grabs me by the collar.

"You're wrong! You never know the 'real' thing that we do! You may think that '360' is only for universities to achieve victories in sports and more." James chuckles.

"Man, that's too rough." James brushes off Tristan's hands off my collar. I just realized about it...Tristan is not so gentleman.

"What a stupid excuse! Those excuses are just to blind the government about the real aim of this society. We all vow to it."

"Tristan, enough, okay?" James gives him a sharp glare. "She hasn't vowed yet!" James said.

"Vow or not, she can't tell anyone about it if she wants to be safe. She's the chief, remember?"

That word stabs me. Why do I feel like Tristan is making fun of me in his tone? It's like a sarcastic word or...jealousy in his words. Had he always been dreaming about being a chief before? When I try to imagine it, Tristan really suits the title well.

"In you go."

I run frantically toward the main door of the antique mansion owned by Aunt Ressa.

"Aunt Ressa!" I barge into the back door of the house which leads to the dim light kitchen. Candles on the bar flickers when I open the door. "Aunt Ressa?"

I hear footsteps coming from the wooden stairs.

"Oh, honey! There you are my little pumpkin!" Aunt Ressa hugs me tightly that I can merely breathe. "Where had you been? Tristan told me that you are fine but not seeing you made me worried. Besides, you left without telling anyone."

Tristan rolls his eyes. "I told you she's fine."

Aunt Ressa chuckles. She then welcomed James. "Have a seat everyone. I had made hot soup for the boys. But, they went to bed early tonight. I also got hot chocolate too."

"Yum..." James grins.

I need to get out of both their sight. "Pardon me, Aunt Ressa, but I really need to use the loo." "Anytime you want, sweetie. This is also your home, remember?"

So, I get up and walk to the hallway. I quickly grab this chance by running toward the main door.

CHAPTER XII

I don't know where my legs had leaded me to. Everything is pitching black. I don't even remember the way to go back to my home. At least I am out of the hell. What a weird dream I had. Just when I was about to reach the main road of the village, someone grabs my hands from behind.

I turn around to meet Aunt Ressa's gaze. Shocked, I hug her.

"Shh…honey, what's wrong. It seems like you are in a really scary nightmare."

"Please don't tell Tristan that I am here. He had brought me to an awful place where I can't escape." Aunt Ressa lets out a small chuckle. Surely she doesn't believe me.

"A place where we are trained like soldier! Please--Let me go home first to father."

"Are you talking about 360?" My eyes widened open. So she knew about it. Of course, Tristan is one of them. Of course she knew.

"I don't want to go there!"

I don't know whether it is my illusion or not, but Aunt Ressa's eyes are changing, from warm to cold and fierce eyes. I shudder in her embracement. "I shall make you return." However, she dragged me to the opposite side of the road, which will lead me back to her mansion.

"NO! STOP!"

"Give it up, mom. She won't listen. Let her escape."

Tristan appears out of nowhere. He is sitting on one of the big tree. James is beside him. They are watching me just like how they are watching their prey.

"I won't let her run away. She is the chief there, right?" I gasp.

"How did you know?" I asked her. Her grip on my arm becomes tighter that it's hurt.

Tristan chuckles. "Unable to answer that tiny daughter of yours?"

"Daughter of yours?" I repeated the words that confused me.

Is there another shocking new awaited for me here?

Tristan shrugs. Aunt Ressa seems to be surprised by his words.

"H—how did you know?" She asked nervously.

Tristan moans. "Secrecy...secrecy...I know. I know everything since the beginning, mom!"

Tristan jumps off from the tree, while James still not moving an inch, seems like he also knew about it.

"Henry's theory was never wrong. In fact, he never missed out any information about his generation." I narrow my eyes.

"Why are you torturing us, mom?" In the dim and chill night, he asked Aunt Ressa with that sorrow look. "I don't understand." Aunt Ressa shakes her head vigorously.

"You know since the beginning that Stellar is going to become a chief of '360', so you switch us, right?"

My heart pounds faster than I can ever imagine. It hurts a lot...

"So, it is. Just as I thought." I look down at the ground. "Tristan suits the title well." Anger and rage are burning in my body! Aunt Ressa is such a big idiot!

"Why did you do that?" I yell at her. Aunt Ressa is taken aback of my action.

"Because of you, I suffered a lot to catch up in the society! You should never do that to me since the beginning! Why do you want me to become the chief? I never want to! You should never switch us! I should live as Tristan by now!"

Aunt Ressa slaps me. "Don't you dare to question every single thing that I did to you! It's for your own sake, Stellar! With this, you'll become brilliant as you live with those brilliant people...And of course you'll get good education as I can't provide one for you, Stellar."

"I AM NOT STELLAR!"

I continue to run…I run and run and run…Until I come to a sudden halt. My head is spinning heavily. Everything is normal, until I enter the base of '360'. That society had turned my world upside down. Everything just because of one single mistake!

I clench my heart. Why, mom? Why switch me? I suppose to be Tristan by now! My name is Tristan Mc'Ashton to be exact! Wait! Not Tristan of course, maybe Taylor Mc'Ashton. Steven is never my brother. The hair color…No wonder Tristan is brunet and I am black. This life…it belongs to Tristan—no. It belongs to Steward, the 'real' Stellar who is living as Tristan back there.

"Enough of grieving, you old fart." I sigh upon hearing that harsh words. "Tristan, I am sorry to take away what yours in the first place. Is that the reason why you hate me?" "Nah…I never dislike you. Besides, I like it this way." My eyes wide open.

"So… You don't mind if I become the leader?" I asked bashfully. Tristan looks at me with sharp glare, maybe he's thinking. "Yeah," he nods.

"And you don't mind if I tell you to keep it as a secret?" "Stellar, I had always kept it for a very long time. Besides, there's no good in me being one."

I walk with Tristan side by side, to the base again. I need to return. Or else I'd being caught fleeing.

"Why did you refuse to become the leader?" "And why did you want to become one?" I ponder upon hearing Tristan's question. "Maybe because I am a cheerleader. And it had been long since I conduct a move."

The wind is chilling... The leaves rustle with each other. I wonder why it takes a long time to go back to 360 compared to go to Aunt Ressa's house.

When I saw the tower of '360', I halt.

"What's wrong?"

"Tristan, teach me so that I can become worth a leader. And that they will never look down on me again." I confess. It's taking a long time for him to respond.

At last, he gave me those twisted smile. "Okay. I will."

I giggle softly

CHAPTER XIII

Time moves really fast in here. It had been a week since I were train to become like them. I have to become like them! Tristan clandestinely taught me how to use gun at night. Now, I knew a little about them.

The guys that wear coats, they are from France.

Tristan explained to me that this pendant—which I was wearing, had a blazing power. It can keep any devices fully recharged without having to wait for a long time. It also gave a high power which can make even a small explosion device like hand grenade goes BOOM, annihilate 10 miles far from the explosion site.

He told me that Henry made this pendant, so that I can protect myself if I was being used to do bad things. He said that it had a secret power in it, which one day, will control me, and he knows how to make that happened. One day...He said one day soon, he can make the pendant to control me without I realized it myself. Okay, that sends me a chill.

How the guys did met the 360? Well, it's indeed a long story. Gwen told me about it.

There's a deceiver once in this society. He's a brilliant person, like the other. Deft, strong and can solve any riddles without needing to think for a long time.

That guy name is Darren. He passed the test by studying all nights, all days... with just one hope, to fulfill his father's wish. His father is the CEO of a massive weapon company where the headquarter is situated in Brest, France. R.E.L.P.H Co. He is the one who stole the pendant, after knowing the power of the pendant.

I just remember that it is the time when dad always bought great devices from R.E.L.P.H Co., I was 15 back then. The company sold out non-rechargeable devices that can last for a very long time. One of it is my watch tracker, which I still used it until now.

Well, the students catch Darren for his crime and stole back this pendant from his father. Mr. Klis, knowing about this, of course become upset and threaten this society.

Now, the aim of this society had altered from creating a perfectionist world into creating a terrorist country filled with youngsters and teens and make us soldiers and sold us with high prices throughout the whole world. Though we knew that we will be taken and sold in any minute, the other are still finding a way to stop them from developing, but no one knows how.

So, they are counting on me... maybe. Maybe they want me to think about a way on how to stop them. Well...

Maybe they can count on me (sigh)… and I can count on Tristan (giggling)…

That's the least that I know.

The full moon shines brightly when Tristan teaches me how to archery. Well, no one is here. They are already gone to sleep.

"I hope you won't disappoint me this time. Chief will always aim right toward the target." I take a deep breath before stretches the bow. I need to hit the bull eye. I NEED TO PROVE THAT I AM WORTHY A CHIEF!

I shot the target…

And… I miss the bull eye by 5 cm upward. I sigh heavily. I am absolutely exhausted already.

"Don't give up yet. Do it again!"

"Tristan…Let's take a break. It's already 12."

"Chief does not take a break! She needs to become strong."

"I am not like you, Tristan. I am only the fake heir, so be gentle in teaching me, okay?" Suddenly, Tristan pulls out a dart and shot it right toward the sleeve of my right arm. It almost hits me!

"Don't you ever say such thing in a public!" I look down to the ground. "I am sorry."

Within a minute, we hear ruffle behind the bushes. I perceive for a long time before a tall guy comes out from his hiding. YUKI!

"Busted!" He shouted.

Tristan rolls his eyes.

"I knew it now why I had lots of doubt about you. You are never once had became one of us. Even with more training and practicing, never once you had the blood like us."

Yuki's words pierce my chest. I just felt like everything around me is foreign. These buildings, practice fields, sceneries, everything in here look at me as an outsider, an intruder. I am not and will never become one of them.

Tristan pushes me aside and stand face to face to Yuki.

"Got any problem with it? You better not open your mouth then," he said while facing each other. Well, Tristan and Yuki did have same height, and their faces are so close to each other.

"Heh. I can't question why chief did it. Beside, chief is the most genius person among all of us, right? I mean by the 'real' chief."

While saying those words, Yuki glances at me with mischievous smirk. He stands arm akimbo right now. Is he trying to threaten me? His eyes said so.

"Okay. That's actually a good plan." Yuki suddenly shouted. I don't get what he means by it. So do Tristan. His eyebrows frown.

"The armies want the chief. So, instead of taking Tristan, we can let them take Stellar instead. They can't do anything once they got Stellar, right? They promised to delete the coordinate of this base if they got our chief, right?"

With shining eyes, Yuki planned. My eyes wide open. If they take me, I will never be able to come back again. Cold sweat runs down my spine.

"What nonsense are you talking about? Leave us now." Tristan ordered. He does seem like a leader now. When he backs herself from

Yuki, he grabs him by the shoulder. "I promise not to tell anyone about it but with a condition." "I knew it already. Let go of me." Tristan snaps his hand away.

Soon, Yuki disappears. I perceive Tristan who is taking a seat on a lion statue. No, he is going to seat on the lion.

Tristan…You're so motivated, unlike me. He doesn't seem to concern about anything. He still looks calm, although we had being busted by Yuki just now. "Continue." His voice had brought me back to reality. I need to show to Tristan that I am as good as him.

The morning comes as usual. It had been 2 weeks since I don't go to school. I also hadn't seeing my dad along this period. Suddenly, I miss him although he is not my real dad. No! Nothing had changed although I had known the truth. Aunt Ressa is not the one who had raised me until I grow up. Dad is the one who had always training me.

But…the chopper sound really makes me froze to death.

Same thing happen. I was unable to move when the chopper almost landed. James pats me from behind. He gives me a warm smile.

"Hey, don't seem so surprised. They are just having a mere visit to our base." He comforted me. But, I am not that stupid to not noticing that they are here for me.

James grabs me by the hand and get into the line. I interfere between his troops. Then, I saw Gwen looking at me. Giving her a big smile, I wave at her. Gwen shows me a motionless face, just like always. Yumiko is beside her; somehow I can see that Yumiko is trembling. And behind them are Joan and John. They are holding hands. What's happening here? Something did seem weird. Or is it just my imagination?

The chopper lands and here comes the same 5 French men. Now, they are wearing white coats. Big smile can be seen from their facial.

"Good day, isn't it?" Alex and Olivia nodded simultaneously.

"Do you have that kid? Oof! The genius beyond the limit." Somehow, I got a gut saying that they are talking about me. 'The genius beyond the limit' eh? It supposes to be Tristan, and you are taking the wrong guy!

"Alright, bring those 4 kids including the chief! We are departing now. You see, we have no time to negotiate anymore. Don't worry; all that you ask for will arrive in a short time, around the day when we will invade that soldier country." The guy said.

Suddenly, the other four men come to grab the students that their leader wants. One of them is me of course. But, the most shocking thing is the other students that being dragged out with me, Yumiko, Joan, Gwen and Zen. You got to be kidding me!

"What the hell do you think you're doing?!" Yuki shouted in rage.

He tries to punch the guy who is dragging his sister, but the other students stop him. When I take a peek at John, he is trembling, clenching his fist so tight.

"We promised you! Don't you remember that, jerk?" Yuki continued talking. Promise? What promise?

The leader chuckles.

"Although you all are genius, sure you all are stupid." Yuki stops to struggle upon hearing his words.

"I never said that I promised. I just nod. Moreover, the agreement is not stated on paper, I forgot to include it." Yumiko shook her head, telling Yuki to stop. "What agreement are you talking about?" I asked him directly. I feel like my fear is not so big compared to my curiosity.

"Well, that bunch of stupid kids there had made agreement. Some sort of—take the chief instead of taking the babies. All I do is nod. Heh- though I never put that agreement on paper. It supposes to be this 2 adults fault for not reading the agreement paper thoroughly." He smirks. That made Yuki glares at Olivia and Alex. So…the kids told them to take the chief in exchange to let those 4 other students go. Now, I just realized how selfish genius can be.

If my friends were in the situation, they will never let them do it. They will find a way so that all of them will not be taken away, including me. Suddenly, I feel so sad. If I had been taken away, there will be no one to come and rescue me. They will surely be relief if they know that Tristan is their own leader, not me. And they will never remember that I exist after all. THIS REALLY UPSET ME MORE!

Then, I saw Tristan grabs Gwen's hand with fierce, which had snap her hand away from the France man who is going to bring her into the chopper.

"Let her go." He said. "What do you think you're doing, kid?" The man asked, but Tristan steps forward with courage and make Gwen moves behind him.

"You said 4 students. 4 are including the leader. If you take her with you, it's mean you are taking 5 students which is not in the agreement, right?"

I bit my lip. So, he just going to let the men take me instead of Gwen? Does he really care so much about Gwen? Then, what about me, his cousin, who had always wanted to be his friend ever since we're little? I look down with a somber feeling.

But, Zen looks calm. He is already been taken away into the chopper.

Yuki grabbed Tristan's collar in rage.

"YOU BETTER DO SOMETHING OR I'LL TELL EVERYONE ABOUT YOUR SECRET!"

Everyone turns to Yuki and Tristan. Luckily the men are busy to take care of the argument as the chopper's blade made a loud noise. Tristan grips Yuki's hands.

"I already took care about it."
"What do you mean by it when you just let them take my sister away?"
"What to be bothered about? They also took my cousin away."
"YOUR COUSIN AND MY SISTER ARE DIFFERENT! Your cousin is useless and dumb and not--."

Tristan punches Yuki's cheeks in an instant. Everyone was shocked and back away from both of them. Yuki stumbles to the ground.

Tristan puts his left leg on his rival's left hand. "You better stick to my plan. Or else, you'll never see your sister alive again!"

He threatened him. Apparently, Yuki just remained silent, being an obedient.

Once again, I was shoved into the chopper. Maybe I am stupid because I actually feeling enthralled to get on the chopper! It's my first time anyway. I was being placed beside Zen. He looks away from me and it had made me wonder why. Why he had been dragged along with me? Why Joan and Yumiko had the same fate as me? Why Olivia and Alex do nothing about the agreement? I am sure that they did that on purpose! I look at Tristan in an instant. He had showed no sign of stopping the men from taking me away. What's wrong with me?

Why I was hoping that he will save me? I know he will never will. Since I am kid, I always rely on him to save me even though he never showed interest in being my friend, or to be exact, I want his attention! I sigh heavily when I think about it again.

"Don't show exaggeration and being so puny!" Zen scolds me suddenly. I glance at him, wondering why he looked so calm. "Why aren't you trembling?" He stares at me with a cold gaze that he never showed before. "I have no one to worry about me, so I don't have any concern about what's going to happen to me." His replied sound like he had always been lonely.

I bite my lip, knowing that I can't calm him, I just keep quiet. After a few minutes, Yumiko and Joan leap into the chopper.

"Geez! These girls are hard to handle with!" One of the men complains. Joan shows a disgust face toward him. Yumiko's face is motionless.

The chopper starts to depart. The men talk to each other in France, I don't understand single word that they said. Zen is already asleep, I guess. He sits up straight with his eyes close. Yumiko and Joan are looking outside the pane, looking a bit sorrow. I can only think about my family now. What will they do if they now that I had flew away from them? Will they be surprised?

CHAPTER XIV

We arrive at the military base. Sure it was huge! More soldiers come to 'welcome' us. I cling Zen as I was scared that they will hurt me. I am still not good in Tae Kwan Do.

They exchange a few words among themselves before guiding us to a huge plain white building. The main entrance leads us into a garage where tanks and trucks are being kept. The man whom they called as Santiano enters a code before the door gate, making it slowly open to reveal a glass door behind it.

The intercom beside the door turns red, but Santiano had said something that made it turn green. We follow him into the main hallway with bright white light.

Santiano leads us to a chamber, with two rooms that only been separated by wall that is half constructed, one for the girls and one for Zen, the only guy here.

"Alright! You stay here until I come and get you again, got it? If you ever try to escape, oooooo…." He shows us a scary face, like we are a bunch of small kids who will be frightened by it. "…You know there are a lot of hidden cameras here. So, beware." With that, he gets out from the room, locking us from inside.

There's long silence… We just sit on the floor in a circle. "Are we…meditating?" I asked hesitantly.

Suddenly, Zen chuckles.

"What do you expect us to do? You are our leader and we are in your command." Upon hearing this, I can feel cold sweat runs down my forehead. Now, all my motivation about wanting to become a leader gone, PUFF…just in a second.

How can I survive in this kind of place?

"Guys, let's just think of something…like how to escape without being seen." I give an idea.

"Uugh…Are you kidding me, chief? Run to where? Please give us explicit details." Joan moaned. I frown, knowing my fault.

"Guys, I know this is not going really well. But, please don't rely on me 100%. I am not good in this yet."

"But, we believe in you, just like how we believe in Henry." Yumiko convinced me.

Sighing deeply, I start thinking about this whole event again. If only I don't know that Tristan is the real heir, if only I don't know that my dad is fake… I am sure that I will have courage to get through all this.

"Um—Even if you all believe in me, you all know how I did this whole time. I never be able to solve anything. I am not… bright as how Henry expected me to. I just—don't. What if I am not the heir? Not your leader?"

Joan pats my shoulder suddenly.

"You are what you think you are. Believe in yourself, no matter who you are, no matter how genius people around you, you got something to show to them that you are not what they think you are. If only you got what I mean." With that, Joan stands up and walks to the near bunk.

"That's deep." Zen smiles to Joan before patting my head and leaves me with Yumiko.

I look at Yumiko with a worried face. I can see that she has no nerve in herself compared to when she was caught earlier. "You're calm."

"Maybe because…I rely too much on my brother that I become weak all of a sudden. I never was being separated from him before. That gave me nerve a bit. But, when you stop relying and think with your own thought, you'll realize that you are not that scared. You have someone with you…Always…think that there's one who always watching you." With that, Yumiko also stands and gets on the top bunk.

I hug my knees tightly, trying to comprehend what Joan and Yumiko had just said. Then, I look at Zen who is tapping the iron desk situated at the edge of the room.

"What if Santiano never come and fetch us?"
"That's great. We have more time to think then." He then sits on the desk with his legs on it too.

When we are doing nothing, suddenly the door is wide open, revealing a beautiful brunette girl with a great body—and husky voice.

"Bonjour, fellas."

***

"Oh?" Zen and I look in amazement upon seeing the girl that is standing in front of the door.

"Yvaine?" I shrieked. Why in the world it must be her? "What are you--."

Eyes in disbelief, I try to approach her when she takes out her hand from her back.

It's Glock17, a gun.

"Back off." Ordering us, we back off a bit. Joan and Yumiko start to look tense when they jump down from the bunk and face Yvaine.

"You, back off!" Joan ordered Yvaine without a nerve.

"Stop! Don't fight here." When I warn both Joan and Yvaine, Yvaine points the gun to me. Is she going nut just because I take her position in ice hockey?!

Suddenly, Santiano comes again, talking to Yvaine in France. After disputing, she turns to me and ogles.

"Just remember one thing. You are in my dad's territory!" With that, she spun around and walks out from the room with her black leather boot that heightens to the knee. I like her boot.

"That arrogant girl, just like her brother!" Yumiko grunts.

"Is she Darren's…"

"Yup." Joan answered haste. Zen still looks in shock.

"I never realize it." He said.

"All this time… she's been watching me…That's why she is in every classes that I attend."

***

I don't know what time it is when the door slides open again. Oh, I had fall asleep without I realized it. "Rise and shine. You'll be working, so hurry up!" A France woman with short tousle dark chocolate hair with black suit come in while ordering through the hailer.

Suddenly, the intercom beside the interior door starts to emit red light.

"YOU'RE BREAKFAST IS READY. PROCEED TO THE CAFÉ."

"You all can hear the instruction given, so move your butt." She said that before leaving the door opens, while holding AK47 at her left hand.

I am at the front, with Joan, Yumiko and Zen behind me. Why are they treating me like this? I don't want to be their leader! When we enter the mentioned café, which is decorated with fake food and lot of dim lights, we saw Yvaine at one of the small round glass table, eating her sandwich.

"You're late…or you're lose?" Ignoring her, we proceed to the a square table that was plastered against the white wall.

"My dad is asking about you all. About how are you doing? Of course I said that you're doing fine. After all, I am the one who chose you." Saying that makes Zen stomps his fist on the glass table, sending it to a crack.

"Zen, calm down." I comforted him.
"You can't do that to us. We're friends!" I yelled at her.
Smirking, she sighs heavily.
"No friends, no mercy." She suddenly jumps up from the table and starts to throw shurikens toward us. I was so surprised that I duck under the table. Only that I realize that everyone did the same thing too.

"Oh?"

"Nice duck!" Joan praised me. Well, thanks. It was unintentional, actually.

Shurikens start to pour down and make the glass break. She jumps toward us from table to table. She got on my nerve when I suddenly hear sword scratching from her belt. She tried to stabs me who is still shaking under the table, but missed it because I roll out from the scene. 'This got to be a dream!' I mused. She keeps attacking Zen. But, they only duck.

"Why aren't you attacking her?!" I yelled at Zen in rage. "'Cause you don't say so!" He screamed while still dodging the sword. "Now, attack!"

With the order, he clenched Yvaine's left hand which is holding the sword with his legs and twisted it, sending Yvaine stumbles on her own body. The samurai sword gets off from her hand. Yumiko does a quick jump and grabs it from the floor. Wow! They are like in movies.

Yvaine lets out a small shriek. Oh, she is going to get up again! She gets up haste, without even look hurt. She throws everything that she can reach, glass mostly, toward me and Zen. She is targeting us ever since! Just then, I saw a glass vase flying toward me. I duck, but not fast enough and the glass breaks into pieces, some pierced my skin.

Joan takes this chance to do a turning kick on Yvaine's head. That will do. But not when someone hits my head from behind. I could not see who as the person is so fast. I hear Zen and Yumiko grunt. My vision is blurred, but I try to fight it as I can't faint at this time!

"Darren, we're not here to fight." That's what I heard Joan said to the guy name Darren.

"How dare you hit my sister?!" "She started it! We are here not to fight, but to work with your dad." With that explanation, they both breaks out from their fighting stance... and the glass door slides open.

CHAPTER XV

"Yvaine, Darren, stop creating problems will you?"

"But, dad…" Darren was trying to say something when Mr. Klis interrupts.

"Enough! This dispute will no longer be extending. Now, dismissed." With that, both Yvaine and Darren walks out from Mr. Klis' office. His office sure is huge. With big arch window situated behind his white work desk, there's sofas in the middle of the room, cream leather sofas, and black glass rectangle table in the middle of it too. On the table, there's a familiar device, the device which had been shown to me when I met the 5 French men for the first time.

"Please, have a seat on the sofa." He invited us, with a big pleasure smile.

After we take our sit, he starts to put his hands together, a sign to start the discussion.

"Well, welcome to my territory. As you can see, its lovely here, isn't it?" He chuckles when we remained silent. "What? Are you nervous about you being sold?" Tapping his thigh several time, he smirked.

"You will never being sold. I never sold the students that I took before. It's just rumors."
"Then, if you don't sell them, where are they?"

Mr. Klis look directly into Zen's eyes. "In my working lab, where they will create new devices for me every day, every time, every hour, every minute and every second!" Answering the question, he looks really satisfied. This bald old man is crazy!

"Then, what are we supposed to do here?" Oops! Maybe I should not ask that question. It sounds stupid!

"What a brilliant question! Because I actually had something for you to solve! You all like solving riddles, right?" I frown. Yumiko and Joan still glaring at him, maybe they are taking tight precautions.

"Look at this." We look at the familiar device on the table. It's so tiny and cute. Like a tiny robot. "This is something that can make me really rich! Do you know what this is?" I shake my head vigorously. "This is the code breaker."

I flinched. Code breaker? When the word code breaker is being said, Zen, Joan and Yumiko's bodies sit straight.
"How?" Joan asked without satisfaction in her eyes.
"Thanks to your dearest soldiers down there! They work really hard to create this one single thing. You know what? This code breaker can hacked any security codes... Hey, and I can also penetrate the militaries' high security codes. I'd test it. It work so good!"

"Then, what are we here for?"

Putting that device down, Mr. Klis clicked his tongue. "EASY. I need four persons to steal the money for me."
"What?"
"Got into the banks, and steal money for me. All you need to do is steal it from a rich bank in the world,"

"We can't, and we will never do that!" I stand up upon hearing his loco idea. "So, you are denying me." "Of course I deny your plan! What do you think you're doing with that lot of money?" Joan shrieked.

Mr. Klis puts his left leg on his right hip and shakes it.
"I want to create a world, full with geniuses, intelligent secret agents. Well, I want to create a country with a perfect military system. Kids and young adults being taught everything about armies. They will march, handle guns, battle and combat like armies. When I finally reach the peak of my success, all other nations will bow to me, making a diplomatic relationship with me… and of course, we'll be rich."

My eyes wide open. "That's an absurd wish! No one will ever let you do that!"

"No one of course, except for a person. You." I step back when his hazel eyes pierce right through me. Me?
"You're the leader, with the highest IQ. I know that you know what to do. Of course the profit will also become yours. You'll not do it for free. I'll pay you."

"I'll call the police!"
When I said that, the door bangs open. And there are again the Klis' kids, Yvaine and Darren. "Even if you call the police, they can't

do anything. We have the most high tech weapons with us compared to theirs." Darren said proudly.

"Father, let me negotiate this time." Yvaine steps forward, looking confident and full with pride. "You accept the job, or else, I boom your base." She tilts her head, looking content. I was so mad! Don't involve the other in this mission!

"We'll see about it!" I said that as I move out from the room, followed by the other.

Now, I am even more motivated to destroy this loco company. Thinking about build new country? They sure are crazy.

"We'll fight! Not outside, but in this same building!" I announced it to my friends behind me. Zen, Joan and Yumiko nod simultaneously.

"That's the spirit, Stellar." Zen said with bloody spirited voice.

I got into the basement, lead by a woman called Sintia. I am so astounded upon seeing there are more workers down there, many sort of ages. Some of them are wearing masks; some of them wear blue uniforms like engineers do. They are like—robot.

When I walk down the marble stair, they all turn toward me. Sintia perceives them and then look at me again.

"Don't do something stupid. Or else, you're finished here." With that, she gets out from the basement, leaving me with the clueless people.

"Hi... I am—Stellar North, Henry's ancestor." After that, lots of whispers surround the basement.

"Alright, guys, listen up. You will help me build a suit that can make me barge into a top security place, like—a bank."

"So, you are following Mr. Klis' plan? We thought you are different."

"I am different! I am not genius like you guys, and that makes me different! Now, stop talking and do that suit!"

Turning around, I give out a deep sigh. "You're doing great, leader." "Thanks." "You're not doing something stupid, aren't you?" The voice shocked me! Ugh- Darren!

"Step away from my work!" I push him aside and walk into the lift. Darren smirks at me. "I'll be watching."

CHAPTER XVI

CLING! CLING!

"Watcha doing?" I turn around to see Zen standing behind me.

"I—uh...doing something."
"What?" He steps closer to me.
"It's nothing. It's just a device that can help me later."
"A device? There's a lot of them." I hadn't sleep. I sneak into the basement to build a device on my own. Well, I end up making 4 devices. I suddenly feel love to create stuffs.

"What is this? It's look like a gun." I quickly snap the small thing away from his hand. "It's uh—Um...A weapon to paralyze someone. I had put a lot of electric in it. Maybe it'll work."
"You haven't tried yet?"
"No. Still in process." Zen chuckles.
"You're quite determined."
"Of course!"

"What's this?" He asked while perceiving 'it'.

"Don't touch it! I am trying to make a bomb! I want to blow this whole place."

"Don't be crazy, Stellar. There are lots of our people in here. You gonna risk all of them if you blow this place."

"I'm trying, okay?" I yell, pushing him out of the room. "Hey, you should go to sleep, okay?" "Got it! Good night!"

No one should disturb me right now because I am planning. I wait for my suit to be ready. And I know it will take lot of time. So, in time being, let's plan an escape first.

After a week of working, at last, my suit is ready.

"Wow! Look at that," Zen said.

"It's so fine!" Joan praises.

I touch the suit. It's really beautiful. The layer is made up of silver leather. I even got myself a black fingerless glove. But there's something inside it that scared me. They had put shurikens inside the glove.

"The suit is invisible in camera, so don't worry."

"What about my face then? They will appear in camera too."

"No worry. This suit will transmit a lot of radar, which will interrupt the camera because of high magnetism. The face will surely appear blurred in camera." The man named Zoey said. "But, it will also affect her, right?" Yumiko said.

"Of course, and people around her too. Once the button is on, the radar will be transmitted. I'm afraid that you had to risk something in order to get something."

"Are you trying to kill me deep down in your heart?" I asked him angrily.

"Of course not, ma'am. I am just trying my best."

"Alright, then. You'll try it first."

"What?"

"Not now of course. I'll give you the specific date and time. Just be alarmed." With that, I step out from his room that is situated near my working room under the basement too.

***

"Are you crazy?" Zoey shouted near my ears and I believe that I'll be deaf in a minute.

"Sheesh! Can you please low down your voice?"

"I just cannot barge in his office right at this moment!" Zoey said.

"Of course you can and you will. Transmit all the data in this hard disk. Everything. I know you know how to hack his computers. And of course, you'll work with your new suit!" I convinced Zoey who seems a bit worried. We are now in my room. Zen is just listening while Yumiko and Joan glance at Zoey.

"You better do that or all of us will be stuck in here, forever!" Yumiko threatened him.

We argue for a long time until Zoey is out of word. "I don't know why you must be our '360' leader!" With that word, he nods slightly and walks out from the room.

"Now, we just have to wait and see." I said. Of course I am a bit happy. Finally, my plan will work.

"Is it okay to use him? I had a bad feeling."

"Do you have plan B?" Yumiko's question gets me back into reality.

"What B?" Gaping, the three of them shake their heads in disbelief.

"We need plan B, if our plan does not go like the way it supposed to be." Tapping my chin, I look at Zen. "Never think about that."

As I was sleeping on the bunk, the door bangs really hard. Joan shakes me hardly, for me to fully awake.

"We gotta have plan B! Plan B! Plan B!" She yelled to Yumiko and Zen also.

"What's happening?"

"Zoey, he's being caught, by Yvaine. Not good! And not cool!"

"All right, plan B. Let's get out of here! And make sure we have all the data transferred. Did he get it?" I asked Joan.

"I think Yvaine got it."

"Then we gotta have it back."

We all wear our black leather jackets, provided by Mr. Klis. It is supposed to be worn when we rob banks but, no time to argue about it. We need to wear anything that we can find HASTE.

I look up, just to find out that the three of them are all ready.

Ready in white suit, we use the code breaker that we found to escape from the coded room. Actually, I stole it from the basement without the soldiers' knowledge. I feel like I don't know which side the soldiers are now.

"Going somewhere?" that voice behind us makes us run even fast. "No use! Plan C!" I yelled at them.

Hearing that Zen moans,

"And what is plan C?!"

No time to answer Zen, we split up. I don't know where to go. But, I was so mad when Yvaine keeps following me! I keep running under the dim light of the long white hallway.

The researchers, scientists and doctors around us give us way; don't want to interrupt the scene.

Suddenly, I feel shurikens hitting my sleeve. Shocked, I stumble on the floor. Knowing that she will bump onto me from behind, I turn my body around to face her.

I dodge my head to the right when I saw her trying to punch me with her left fist.

Unable to hold her weight on me, I punch her stomach with all my might. Of course she doesn't gets up, only stumbles back a bit. This is my chance to kick her head. As I did that, she gets off from me, and I run away frantically.

But, easy said than done. She grabs my right leg, making me bumps hardly on the floor—again.

That's when I saw Yvaine twisting a knife on her hand. This is bad!!!

I quickly kick her hand, wanting her to let go of the knife. But, I missed her hand and accidentally kick her front pocket of her jacket.

That's when the most vital thing drops out from there. The hard disk! Wow! Her pocket sure is big.

I want to take it, but Yvaine fettered my legs, making me unable to move.

"Get off me!" I try to kick her, but she is just too strong.

A woman, with black hair, and fair skin, picks it up and runs somewhere else.

"STOP!" I yell.

"Yamete kudasai!" Yumiko yells while running toward the woman, who is running in her black heels. Yumiko sends her a flying kick, making that France woman grunts and falls. She slides on the slimy floor and snatches the hard disk away.

Without looking back, she runs away from the hallway. Thanks to that, Yvaine's attention turns toward the Japan girl.

Alright, plan C… plan C… What's plan C? Bombing!!!

I shake my head vigorously. I will hurt the other too. But… I think, the researchers and the others down the basement is no longer 360. I think that their loyalty had turned toward Mr. Klis.

So that's what I decided to do, bombing. I pull out 5 bombs that I made myself from my pocket.

Made my way to the basement, I met Zen. Oh God! His body is full of wounds.

"Darren's fault. He doesn't want to let me through," he explained without I need to ask him.

His cheek is bleeding great, so do his black jackets. There's a slash torn on it.

"Why not use gun to kill you?"

"Good question. I kick it from him just before he pulls the trigger." We enter the lift and go down to the basement.

"Alright, we'll bomb this place, starting from here. Then, the infirmary and beside it, the labs. Second, we'll go toward Mr. Klis' main office. Use the code breaker to barge in the room." Zen nodded, running into the basement. He steps down the round stairs when he met lot of former 360. Seems like they know what we're planning to do, they make a row along the way, not wanting us to enter.

"You better step back, Stellar. You are no longer in your territory, and no one will listen to you." A man wearing spectacle said. Just as I thought about the people in here.

"Throw this now!" Without warning, I hand Zen the hand-made bomb and make him throw it far into the basement. All the people start panicking, running around frantically and squeezing into the lift. I was so shocked with that reaction.

"Oh...I never thought about what will happen next." I said to Zen. I also squeeze through the crowd but I see that Zen is not moving even an inch.

"Zen, we gotta get out of here!" I yelled at him.

That's when I see that he is glaring at me.

In a second, the basement is empty. I can feel wind chilling through my skin as I look at the lift that is moving upward.

"What is this?" Zen's question snaps me back into reality.

"What's wrong?" "Your bomb, it's not even exploding. It only produces sparkle." He said with arm akimbo.

CHAPTER XVII

I never thought that my plan didn't work.

What a shame!!! Zen scratches his head which is not itching.

"Yeah. And how do we annihilate this place without bomb?" Zen asked. I grin stupidly.

"I never thought about that. I should think thoroughly about it." I said. Zen sighs heavily. Well, I told him not to rely too much on me.

"Let's get into the weapon storage. At this hour, the factory might be packaging weapons right now. So do hand grenade. We can get hand grenades from there!" Zen suggested.

"But it's not easy. We must get out of this huge building in order to get to the factory. I think there will be high security around this building." Zen shakes his head. He pulls my hand and get into the lift that just comes down again.

We look around before escaping the lift.

"Go, go, go!" I follow Zen from behind. When we about to encounter one of the worker in the building, we hide in between the wall. There are small gaps at every section of the hallway, allowing us to hide in between it.

Suddenly, I saw something that makes me nervous. The security camera above us is turning red. In 5 seconds, alarm starts to rise. "This is not good." Unwillingly, we run toward the main gate. And we encounter lot of guards, wearing soldier suits. Or maybe they are soldiers.

"We need guns." Zen whispered to my ears. I hand him a gun that I made myself, the one that can paralyze people. Zen, without thinking, points the gun toward the guards that is assembling at one of the door that will lead us to the main entrance. He pulls the trigger and—

"Zen?" I shake his shoulder, but he is not moving an inch. Knowing that the guards had realized our presence behind the wall, I pull Zen away from the wall with all my might. I look at Zen and saw that he is frowning.

"Don't move!" The shouts make me even more shudder. Not knowing what to do, I pull Zen hard and that makes him stumble, with his body still not moving, like a paralyze robot. "I am so sorry for not testing the gun first."

As I was protecting Zen from behind, I heard gunshot. I close my eyes, knowing that the guard is shooting at us.

CLING.

As soon as I heard metal cling, I open both my eyes and turn around to see Joan and Zoey holding metal barriers, a big silver metal barriers. After the gunshot stop, both of them throw the barriers toward the guards, making them stumble backward.

We take the chance to pass through the guards and get into the room that is connected to the main entrance. Zoey is there to piggy back Zen.

With both Zoey and Joan help, we manage to get into the factory through the backdoor.

"You're really killing me, Stellar." Zen said. At last!

"I am so sorry for making you paralyze. I never thought that the gun will fire backward."

"Ugh- Are you really are the leader? You seem to not using the brain correctly." Zen scolded me.

When he said that, I took a step backward. All of them stare at me, looking puzzled. "What's wrong?" Zoey asked.

"Of course I am the leader! Can't you see that all my plans work so far?"

Joan shrugs before make a way into the factory. I am sure is lying to myself. In this kind of situation, I should just be honest with them so that they don't rely on me so much. But, I just can't. I want them to see me as a leader. I want to command them!

The lies in me, I want it to keep going! I am the worthy leader for them! Not Tristan!

"All right, come!" I lead them. All I need to do now is take some explosives and some guns…though I am not still good in using them.

It is so dark that I keep stepping on Joan's legs when we walk. "Watch your step, please!" She said half whispering. When we saw a light, we make a cautious move toward it. Then, we saw a huge machine, in the centre of it!

We follow to where the machines move the gun to. The workers in there seem to not knowing what's going on outside. They are like living in their own world. The sirens that rise did not even bother them at all.

We finally make our way to the packaging section where guns are being wrapped. As we only need few guns, I only take two guns with me, along with the ammos. Well, Zoey helps us stole them from one of the box when the worker is not looking.

I picked one that I can handle easily, the desert eagle.

Then, we made our way to explosion packaging. Proximity mine, hand grenades, flashbangs, C4s... We take everything that we can, and feel it into Zoey's new suits. I also put some in my pockets, I mean the C4s of course.

After we finish it, we run out to where we come.

Not when there are a lot of people waiting us outside, and at the front row, I can see Yvaine, Darren and Mr. Klis, ready in combat suit.

"No way!" Zoey yelled.

"It seems that you already forget the cost of your action." Yvaine started to talk.

Just then, I remembered that she will bomb our base if we try to do something stupid. Knowing what will happen; Zoey makes a drastic plan by throwing down his weapon, and takes off his suit. "Don't do that, Zoey!" I warned him, but he seems to be ignoring me.

Darren smirks. "This coward. That's what I like about you ever since we're friend. Thanks for being so loyal to me and my family." He said. Knowing that there's nothing we can do, we surrender.

CHAPTER XVIII

We had been lock up in the jail situated at the abandoned site of the main building. It is really dark, abandoned, filthy and a bit smelly. The floor is a bit chilly and the ceiling seems to be leaking. There's lot of mud on the floor, well I am not sure where it comes from.

"Don't worry; we'll get that Japanese for you." Yvaine said while smiling with content.

I wonder what happen with her and the hard disk.

***

TWITCHING...TWITCHING...TWITCHING...

Stellar frowns. Something's hurting her head. It's really hurt that Stellar falls onto the floor, gasping for air. No one realized... no one ever think of waking up in the late of the night, and not knowing what is happening to Stellar.

She clenched her head with tight grip. And in a moment, she stops struggling.

The awakening…

"Stellar, Stellar… Wake up! It's almost 5. We should be getting out of here." Joan shakes Stellar's body vigorously. Stellar rubs her eyes and scratches her head. Her hair gets all messy; surely she is having a good sleep.

"How do we get out of here? Our code breaker had been taken away." Zen said in rage. "All my guns also! Thanks to you, Zoey!" He starts to grab Zen's collar and lifts him up when Stellar hushes them.
"No worry. I got something."

She gets up and clings herself onto the jail door. She whistles and whistles and whistles.

"Will you stop that, Stellar? It's irritating me!" Joan scowled.
Then, a tough biceps guard with soldier uniform comes and bangs the jail door with his hand. "Will you stop it?! You are hurting my head!"

But, with a flash, Stellar grabs the guard by his collar with all her might. As the guard didn't expect that, he is not ready and accidentally hits the jail door with his head. To confirm that the guard is sure in pain, Stellar kicks him at the forbidden zone using her right knee. He contorted in pain, while holding his 'thing'.

Zen and Zoey seem to be grimacing.

With that, Stellar takes the gun from his chest pocket and puts it on his forehead.

"Open the door, or else, I shoot you. You choose your life or your freedom!"

The guard's loyalty toward Mr. Klis had prevented him from moving, pretending to be in so much pain that he doesn't move even an inch. Stellar shoots his leg, making him jumps a bit, frightened.

Without any word, he opens the door. Once he did that, Stellar takes out her paralyze gun and points the back of the gun toward the guard. She pulls the trigger and the guard starts to black out.

"That will hold him for a bit."

Zoey looks at Stellar with a great puzzle. A backfired gun? That gives him idea to create something new next time.

"Hurry up, Zoey!"
"Ouh, sorry."

As they run out from the dark place, the bright light is hurting their eyes. As Stellar's vision is clearer, she can see a familiar body in front of her…Yumiko.

"Yumiko, there you are. We should get out of here." Joan is approaching her when Stellar grabs her hand.
"What's wrong?"
"She is not her."

As Stellar said it, Yumiko starts to jump high and do a flying kick toward Stellar but she managed to dodge.
She throws her friends the C4s that she hid it in her inner jacket.

"Bomb this place. C4 can annihilate this whole place. High explosive." Seeing the C4, Yumiko starts to grab it, but her movement is fettered by Stellar, who has kicked Yumiko's leg, making her fall hardly on the white tile floor.

Zen can hear them fighting from the distance.

"Something's wrong with Stellar. She's being—genius." He started to talk about what he had observed. "No difference. She is still commanding like always." Zoey disagrees.

"No. Zen's right, whenever she gave orders, she always sound so doubt, but still we had to listen, because she is our leader. But now, I can feel the real leader in her."
"Maybe because of her confidence in giving order."
"Whatever it is, I am glad that she had come to her consciousness. Now, we can rely on her."

The three of them nod at each other and run to their destination.

"Well, looks like you are not yourself." Yumiko starts to speak after having a rough time sparring with Stellar.
"And so do you." Stellar replied. Yumiko starts to walk around Stellar, observing every inch of her body.
"It's been a long time…Tristan!"

After hearing the name, Stellar quickly kicks Yumiko's face but, she dodges it and in the meantime, she kicks Stellar right onto the stomach. Stellar grunts.

"You're bright enough to notice, Darren." Stellar replied.
"Ha! So you noticed too. Well, Tristan, the coward. Why are you hiding in a girl's body? Are you unable to confess that you are the truly heir of this illegal organization?" Stellar clenches her teeth.
"I know what I am doing. And you don't have to know."
"Well, it's just so obvious that this girl is dump, slow and stupid."

"At least, she can fight in her own way."

"Which is not working. That's why I was able to catch them whenever they tried to flee. But still, she keeps acting like she is the one, the genius. Such a huge lie."

"Stealing the power of the pendant is quite a dirty work, deceiver."

"And so do you, cheater."

With that last word, they keep fighting and fighting.

The three of them walk into the basement which seems a bit astray. Maybe because the other had evacuated the basement ever since they thought the basement really is being destroyed.

"Plant it at the middle of this room. I am sure the effect will be great." Zen suggested. "Well, she gave us 2 C4s. I am sure that this will be great. One at this basement, one at the main control tower."

"Control tower?" Joan looks at Zoey, wanting more explanation.

"Do you see that another tall building besides this main building? It's a control tower, which is being connected by Mr. Klis' office. There's a secret door at Mr. Klis' office. That door will lead us to a high tech bridge which connects this building with the tower. I don't see another way to get there instead of using Mr. Klis' room." Zoey explained and the other nod.

"Finished planting?" Joan nods slightly before making their way to the tower. "We need to stop Yumiko and Stellar first!" Zen warned. There's no way he can let the other two stuck in the building with the other Mr. Klis' followers!

There are so many wounds on Stellar's body and Yumiko also. "Stellar, enough of fighting her!" Joan shots Yumiko at her thigh which shocked Stellar. Seeing that Yumiko is in pain, Stellar punches her, making Yumiko lose her consciousness. With that, Zoey starts to piggyback her.

"Where are you planning to go?" Stellar asked.

That's when other soldiers start to come to their way. Stellar shoots all the security cameras and also the soldier that is marching toward them.

"Nice shot." Zen praised her.

"We're going to the tower to plant C4 in there. Girls, you should make your way out of this building!"
"No! Not without the hard disk." Stellar protested.
"But, we need you to get out of here, safely."
"What about Yumiko? She is still under control." Joan asked.
"Don't worry. After this building had been exploded, Yumiko will regain her sense as the controller is also exploded in there." Stellar said. She takes Yumiko from Zoey's back.

"Joan please gives her a piggyback. I am going to get that hard disk back." Then, Zen points the gun toward Stellar. He pulls the trigger and it shot the soldiers behind her.

"Thanks." She said.

"We need to move fast." Zen said. "Quickly get out of here after you plant the bomb." Stellar ordered. "And you too. Here, take this gun. And this ammos." Stellar shoves the armor into her pocket and runs away from there.

Joan makes her way to the main entrance with Yumiko on her back. Zen and Zoey make their way into Mr. Klis' office to go to the tower.

Stellar wanders around the main hallway quietly, looking back and forth in hope to meet Yvaine. The sound of soldiers' boots rushing toward her makes her got into one of the unlock room which is so pitch black and she can't see a thing.

She lights on her watch, just to see something that enthralls her.

The soldiers grunt after shurikens hit them. Stellar rolls happily in her new found roller skate. She skates in the main hallway, to find the person that she always wanted to see, Yvaine.

"There you are."

"And there you are too, Tristan. Darren told me about you and you should not hide that from me. It's an honor to meet the leader of 360."

Yvaine bows down before starts to throw shurikens toward Stellar. With every hit, she dodges it with her legs by kicking all the shurikens.

"You're good, not like that fraud leader." As Yvaine spoke that, Stellar rolls haste toward her and slides through the tiles to kick Yvaine's legs, sending her to a loud bump.

"Sorry for not being gentle. Now, tell me, where's the hard disk."

"Like hell I'll tell you!"

With that answer, Stellar pulls Yvaine blonde hair and squeezes it tightly.

"TELL ME!"

Yvaine grunts, clenching her teeth in order to hush herself.

Gunshot…

Stellar eyes' wide open. Slowly, she closes her eyes and falls down. Darren had shot her down.

"I told you I can handle her."

"She's not her, she's him. Get the other 3, including Zoey."

Darren and Yvaine run away from the scene, leaving the fainted Stellar.

Chapter XIX

I shook my head several times. Oh! It's hurt!!! I feel like just hitting my head on a hard rock.

When I was about to stand up, I feel a really quite painful pain at my stomach. So, I touch it, only to feel dark liquid pour down from it.

Oh no! I'd being shot down, but by whom? Why am I out of the prison? When did I make my way here? And—why am I in roller skate?

I grunt as I can't get up, it's aching a lot. All I want to do now is to lie down and sleep a little bit as my vision got blur and more blur.

"Stellar! Stellar! Get out of there!" I try my best to open my eyes and regain my consciousness. "Who's talking to me?" I questioned. That voice sound familiar.

"Stellar, you need to get out of there. Zen and Zoey had planted bombs in the building and it will explode within 30 minutes from now!

"Unable to move, I ignore the voice.

"Stellar! Wake up! You're gonna die!"
"Sheesh! Who's talking to me?!" I cried back. What an annoying voice. Can't he see that I am so much in pain?

Just then, I recall back.

"Tristan?"
"Stellar, gets up and moves out from there. I am serious now."

Tristan... I don't know why but I don't want to hear his voice. He'll never come to rescue me. Annoyed, I take off my pendant and push it aside. Now, there's no more voice calling me. As I continue my sleep, I feel like my body is being lifted. Oh?

As I feel like I am getting weaker, I ignore whoever is carrying me...And so, I close my eyes.

***

"Stellar?" lights flickered into my eyes as I heard a sweet voice girl called me. "Hmm?" I try to have a good look around, but my eyes seem to get heavier.

"She's awake." I know that voice.
"Yumiko?"
"Daijoubu." She said while holding my hand.

She's mean by 'its okay', maybe knowing that I was still scared. I touch my stomach, just to feel a bandage around it. "Where are we?"

I asked around. "Far away from R.E.L.P.H. Co." "Where's Yvaine, and Darrel, and Mr. Klis?" I asked Zen, Zoey, Joan and Yumiko.

"Well—we don't make it. We don't find the hard disk, but I bet that it also exploded along with the building." Zoey said.

"You're lucky I get you in the first place. I told you to extract the building immediately." Zen said and his face seems a bit concerned.

"I am sorry." I bow and apologized.

"And where are we now?"

"Guipavas."

"Guipavas? Just where is it?"

My clarion question makes them look at each other, with frown on their eyebrows.

"The old Stellar is back. Just where did all your genius go?" Joan asked with irritation.

"It's near to Brest. Only take 15 or 17 minutes to reach here."

"And what are we doing in Guipavas?"

"Hello, we're running away, remember? Far from the explosion." I nod vigorously. It's almost dawn. The sky is beautiful, with dark blue but still filled with stars that brighten the sky. I can even see the moon. It's been a long time since I get to see the view. It had been almost a month since I am connected to this organization. What's happened now? I don't know. Maybe I had passed the test? Maybe I need to practice playing and sparring some more? Or...maybe I need to spend all my life forever in the base of 360.

I only need some time to feel the relaxation after being engaged with that society for a—long time I must say. I hadn't seen the outer world for a long time.

"Well, I must say that you all are hungry. Let's get a food at... Well... It's still early. No restaurants open at this hour." Zoey said.
"What about your home?" Joan asked. Surely she is starving.

"Sorry. But, I got no home. That building just now is my home. Mr. Klis provided us with homes, just in another basement."
"You're saying there are a lot of basements in there?"
"Two to be precise."
"Two?"
"One is the place where we design and created electronic gadgets where you had been to. Another one is under the main entrance. That's where we live."
"I don't see any way to get there."

"Of course you won't. Its entrance is behind the wall and its super secret. I bet it all collapsed into pieces in the explosion." Zoey explained to us while walking on the country road.

"Then where did the other go when the explosion happened?" I asked curiously.
"I'm scared that they are hiding at their homes. They're going to die." I said worriedly. That's when we take a halt.
"We should go back to check whether they are safe or not."

"No, Stellar. It's the only way to stop Mr. Klis from using the '360' students. Maybe he'll not mess around with us anymore. And he maybe he will stops creating weird gadgets that'll only bring chaos and annihilation to countries." Zen said hesitantly.

"But, the workers are just innocent here. We can't kill them all just because they used us. They create weapons to be sold out... And the weapons are used by soldiers to protect the country."
"What's gotten into your head? You're the one who want us to bomb that place in the first place." Yumiko started to get mad.

Then, I come to my sense. "Oh...I totally forget about it."

"We did a great job back there, Stellar. You also did a great job by giving us the orders." Zen said while patting my shoulder.

"If we don't stop those guys, another new extreme military world will exist. With this destruction, that can slow down their pace and we can think of another way to stop them if they don't want to give up yet." Zen explained.

I nod again. Wow. I just make a great decision back there.

"Well... Let's walk to the restaurant. We just have to wait until a restaurant open and we can walk into it."

"Do you have money with you?" Yumiko's question makes Zoey gasps.

"Oh...I'm afraid that I totally forget about it." Our shoulders slump.

"Haha. I bet you all are hungry."

"Famished." The three other replied that simultaneously, but I am the only one who said, "Starving."

"You know another trick to get money?" Zoey asked. All of us shake our heads. He held out a code breaker.

"I got this."

"Even if you got that, you still don't have a bank card." Zoey showed Zen a disgust face upon hearing those reply.

"I always have this with me. Ta-da!" We tilt our head, observing the card.

"This is called stealing."

"Whose bank card is that?" I asked curiously.

"No worry. We just had to take out the money." And so, that's how we got our cash at this France city. I never know that Guipavas is has a really beautiful scenery, I only know about Paris back there.

First of all, we ate ice cream to endure our hunger… and have a walk with the morning breeze. But, I think it's awkward to walk with them. They don't have a sense of wanting to have a relax time.

"Zen, stop perceiving around! You look like a spy who is peeking on someone."

"I do?"

"Yeah, Yumiko. Please don't glare at those kids."

"What? They are looking at me. It's kind of uneasy."

"Maybe because you're Japan. You had a different figure from all of us." Ignoring me, Yumiko sighs and looks away.

"Joan?"

"What?"

"Don't clean that knife here." I take away that knife from Joan's hand

. "Hey!" She tried to take it away from me.

"Just had a normal life for once you guys."

"We know how to be normal, okay?" Zen answered me.

"Ah~~ It's open…" We look at each other. "Le Ship Inn?"

"Well… I like to come here to eat." Zoey said with a satisfied face.

"Well…we got to follow the expert." And so…we fill our empty belly in there.

As we're eating, folks come and take a sit behind us. They are chatting with excitement. But, at some moment, Zen and Zoey stop eating.

"What's wrong?" I asked them.

"Nothing." Zen replied.

"Like hell nothing is wrong when you show us that face." Joan scowled, madly.

"I'll tell you later."

And that's was our very first delicious meal in France. Better than that breakfast from R.E.L.P.H. Co.'s breakfasts, lunches, dinners and suppers.

CHAPTER XX

"That folks are talking about R.E.L.P.H. Co. building."

"Oh, really?"

"Wow, Zen, you understand them?" Zen ogles at Yumiko.

"Of course I am. I learnt a lot about France. They're speaking Breton."

"Breton? Never heard about it." I said. Zen immediately punches my head lightly.

"Of course you don't. You never get to learn much, aren't you? Though I am curious why you are acting so full of leadership back then."

"I am?" I asked in surprised and I am amazed by myself.

Zen nods hesitantly. "Well, maybe because I don't rely much on someone anymore." I said happily.

"Yeah. And let yourself die in that explosion. That's what we called self independence. I can see that you already surrender yourself in that building." Zoey butted in.

"It's just that--." I sigh heavily. I hate to hear Tristan's voice, and that's make me surrender to live anymore.

Then, Zoey walks away.
"Where are you going?"
"Buying some news." He waves to us without even looking back and walk straight towards a small shop where an old lady is waiting. They seem like to know each other for a long time. I narrowed my eyes as the wind is getting stronger. We are sitting in the bench, waiting for the newspaper boy (Zoey).

"Okay. I got it here." Zoey comes, like a child who just got his candy.

"Are you a kid, who runs frantically with a newspaper on your hand?" Joan asked lazily.
"Hey, I am 25!" he snapped. Yumiko snickered at him as she makes some space for him to sit.

"What did he said, reporter?" Zen asked impatiently. Zoey clears his throat and starts to read the newspaper out.
"Oh, boy, in English, please." Joan snapped him.
"Sorry."

"'Explosion in Brest, along with the death of a successful... owner of R.E.L.P.H Co.'" Zoey's voice sounds sad. Well, after all Mr. Klis had been taken care of him ever since he abducted him.

"He died in the explosion, trying to protect something that is also destroyed in his arms. 190 workers found dead...98 with bad injured, and 2 with small injuries. Other workers had fled from the scene before explosions could occur." Zoey halts.
"Did they say something about Mr. Klis' kids?"

"No... Let's see." He reads the whole news silently before starts talking again.

"It didn't say anything about teens."

"Maybe they could not find one."

"But, how do we get back to United State?" That question is a major question of the day. Hmm...How?

"Oh, Stellar, you drop this, right?" Zen held out the crimson pendant.

Oh. I totally forget about it. I take the pendant from his hand.

"Well, chief. Don't just leave your property on the ground. It's dangerous." Zoey warned me.

"Guys...is it okay to pretend as your chief right now?" I asked.

"Why not? You had always being our chief." Zen said with a broad smile. Yeah... Although it is truly a lie from me...

Just then, my watch beeps. Huh? I look at it in puzzlement.

"What's this?"

"Oh? Why aren't you telling me that you had the latest R.E.L.P.H Co.'s watch?"

"Don't tell me that is DiGi15 watch!" Everyone seems surprise.

"Well, it's a present from my dad when I was 16."

"Do you know what the function of this watch is?" I shake my head at Joan's question.

"I only know that it tells time and there's tracking device in it."

I keep silence for a while. Tracking device? So, my dad will know where I am now, right? Suddenly, my eyes lit up. I feel very elated right now.

But, won't he be mad if he knows that I am in France?

"This will do." Yumiko takes off my watch even though I don't give her my consent. Then, she connects it with a device, like a map…that shows coordinate… and… It's a small computer that fit in your pocket.

"This is called GPMobile." She started to explain.

"It can be connected to a tracker device…and makes a call at person who is watching this tracking device now."

"You mean—only if the person watches the tracking device of this watch?" Yumiko nods.

"It's not so efficient. But, it's better than not having cell phones with us."

"Definitely." Zen agreed with Yumiko. Without hesitation, Yumiko puts the earphone that is connected to the GPMobile at her ears. Her black hair sways forth due to the wind, which seems a bit pretty. She tied her long hair neatly on the left side.

"Oh… You're watching?" Silence. She is talking with someone on the GPMobile.

"Oh? You're nearly there? Okay…" As she hung up, she looks at us.

"Well, someone is coming over here with a chopper. We should wait at Brest." Yumiko informed.

"What? I am not going to Brest again."

"You wanted to be extracted or not?"

"Who's going to pick us?"

"We just wait and see." Yumiko said while leaning on the wooden bench.

"Hey, we should get going now!" I yelled at her.

"No worry. Brest or not, they'll pick us up here, because the tracking device said so." All right, here's come the arrogant Yumiko.

After several minutes waiting, chopper arrives exactly above us. The Guipavas people look at it in amazement. Of course it not gonna land on here. So, they drop ladder rope for us to climb on. We get into the chopper one by one. And of course I'll be the last person because I need to focus on my 'babies' first before mama comes up.

But...I... NO!

In the chopper, Tristan gives me a cold gaze. I bit my lip and take a sit beside Zen where Zen is sitting in front of Tristan. Seeing this, Zen exchanges his sit with Zen, which makes me a little uncomfortable.

Being beside him is not my dream!

"What the hell did you think you're doing?" He asked, and I can sense that he is holding his voice. I look outside the window, avoiding his gaze and question.

"Oh, so you're avoiding me now after trying to suicide in that building?" He asked again, but this time in a higher tone.

"And what do you care?" I asked him. Even though my voice is low, I don't know how Tristan can hear it in the loud wind.

"You think that I don't care?! Of course I care! You're my family after all." I tend to look away again. Just stop talking to me!

"And what's wrong with you all of a sudden?" he asked again, pushing my shoulder so that I will face him. I keep ignoring and look elsewhere. What am I doing? I am acting just like a child.

"Sorry. I'm fine." At last, I said and then drop my head on the chopper's body. I just need a nice sleep right now.

***

As we arrive at the base, more people are waiting for us. *"Onee chan!"* Yumiko shouted while running toward Yuki. Yuki looks really pleased with Yumiko's presence. John is also searching for Joan and embraces her the time he saw her.

James shakes Zen's hand and more people come to surround us. I sigh as no one seems to care about me. Alex and Olivia are so pleased to see Alex. They keep laughing and chatting like old pals. I step away silently from the place. As I don't know where to go, I get into the Wing Building and into Gwen's room, which is also mine.

I meet Gwen once I open the door.

"Hello. Welcome back." She greeted me. I was so shocked when she stood up and hugged me. "I was so worried."
"Why would you be worried?"

"Because you're not supposed to be abducted from the French men. But, I bet you got lot of experiences from there." I sigh as I remember the day when Tristan saved her instead of me.

"You look sad." She said. Well, Gwen is being a little gentle. I wonder what'd happened. "Why did Tristan saved you that day?" I gained my curiosity to ask her.

"Well…He is always acting like that with me." She chuckles.
"And why is that?" I asked with jealousy.
"Well… maybe because he feels indebted with me. I did saved him once when the French men was about to take him."
I was shocked upon hearing that confession.
"When?"

"He was 16 back then. He shows great achievements in everything that he did. He is so good, in everything. Should I call him a perfect man? I am so in love with him that moment. So, I keep spending some time with him."

Suddenly, Gwen's face turns somehow, bitter.

"Then, the French men came to take him away. Knowing that he would go, like the other did, I gripped his arm tightly. I even kicked them to stop them from taking him away. All I know is that he'll not be taken away." She sighs.

I never thought that he is so much in debt with me because of this.

"Are you coupling?" I asked curiously. Seeing my eyes, Gwen's eyes wide open.

"Do you—like him too?"

Oops…Bull eyes! "O—of course not! I was just asking. Well, of course I wanted to know how do you feel about him and what's your relationship with him."

"Well…he did treated me nicely…But I don't know whether it's love or…because of my debt to him." She looks down the tile while playing with her toes. So that's it…

To think about it—Gwen really suits him well. It's not possible for him to like her.

It's night when I walk out onto the high platform of the Wing Building. Well…I locked myself in there until night fall. I just don't want to meet anyone today.

There, I can see stars and the beautiful dark skies. I can also feel the chilling air. "Hey." Someone admonished me. When I turn around, I saw Tristan, in his blue knee length short and a cyan round neck shirt, with Adidas logo on it. His hair is quite messy, maybe just gets up from a long nap.

He sits beside me, really close that I take a step away.
"Don't do that."
"Do what?" I asked, pretending not to know.
"Avoiding me,"

I ignore him and put my chin on my knees.
"I am not."
"Yes, you are."

There's a long silence…

"I am sorry if I hurt you." At last, Tristan starts to talk.
"You never did that." I said, half whispering. I tighten up my pink sweater.
"I am sorry for not protecting you too." When he said that, he looks away. Okay… That's awkward.

"And I am sorry if I protect Gwen instead of you, if that's what you are upset about." That last words stab me. I am upset, but he not needs to know.

"How's your wound?" I give him a bitter smile. "I'm okay now." Then… we keep silence again… "Sorry for not being honest." "About what?" I look at him. He's not being honest about what?
"Maybe if I am not one of 360, I can be more honest." With that word, he gets up and lefts me alone on the platform.

CHAPTER XXI

"Let's greet our 360 leader, Stellar Victoria North."

The 360 students give a round applause to me as I walk on the stage. Here we are, gathering in the basement again that was constructed under the sky cracked building.

"Thanks for…teaching me many things. I just realize how stupid I was when I am living with you guys. But, I manage to become the best now, right? And also, thanks to Mr. Klis for taking me to Brest, France. There, I had learnt many things and I had done many things. Maybe I am not suited to be your leader, but I promised that I am always your leader and no one can change that fact." I bit my bottom lip after saying that.

Yes…This title is mine. The leader is me.

With that word, Olivia comes toward me and hands me a scroll. I open it up, and start to read the oath.

"I vow to become one of the 360 and being loyal to it until death separates me from my life. I will always served to 360 with all my heart, and I vow to keep this organization a secret from authorities as I will not repeat the same mistake that Henry North did the first time this organization is being built. I, Stellar Victoria North, will also vow to always being a great leader that will think of ways to help this organization to move forward and fulfill the dream of our ancestor, which is to create a perfect world."

With that, I had vowed to become one of the 360, and I am free to roam around without being locked in this place.

After a several days, I go to university as usual. But, now, I seem to be able to catch up a bit with the learning.

Weekend arrives, and I wasn't thinking of going to Aunt Ressa's house right now. Instead, I go to a river in a cottage near my house. There, I saw Tristan, doing something. I approach him slowly and give him a small smile. After the incident, we still talk to each other but...we rarely fight about things.

"What are you doing?"

"Something. There's one mission left." He said. I look around him. It's look like a bomb. I open the boxes near him.

"What is this?" My eyes wide open when there is a lot of bombs in here.

"Are you trying to destroy our country too?" I asked him curiously.

"Did you remember what I told you? About Albert Einstein..."

I nod slightly.

"What's with it?"

"The bomb formula, $E=mc^2$. The formula that the genius Einstein created unintentionally..."

"Is that the reason why you told me about the annihilation?"

He is mixing some mixtures. I really am curious now. "Just watch and learn." He said. Then, James appears out of nowhere with Kimble.

"Are you ready?" Tristan nods slightly before making his way into James' van.

"Where are we going?" I asked them but, they aren't saying anything. It's creeping me out.

Then I realize where are we heading to, the base of 360. "Oh, we're here! I really miss Gwen!" I was about to jump out of the van when Tristan stops me.

"We're here not for visiting session." James said. That's shocked me! So they are trying to destroy this base!

"No! Don't kill them! Just don't!" I hug Tristan, fettering him from getting out of the van.

"Hey! Let go of me!" He struggles away from my arms, but of course I am not letting him go.

"Stellar, we know what we do." James tries to comfort me. Slowly, I let go.

Tristan touches my shoulder, making me facing him. "I know the consequences of having this organization. And I know what will happen if I don't do this, But, you mustn't come. Stay here! I MEAN IT, because after this, everything is up to you, whether to proceed or..," Tristan said while holding the pendant on my neck. "Take good care of this too, '360' leader."

I watch them run down the hill and into the base.

So, I sit down, watching from far away while hugging me legs tightly.

Suddenly, I hear explosions, a lot of explosions. I quickly stand up, worrying about Tristan.

I CANNOT WAIT! Haste, I run down the hill and into the base! So many smokes in here! Strange, it's a purple smoke. I close my nose because I can't inhale this bad smell!

Later on, my vision starts to recover. I can see clearly now. Oh?

No buildings are destroyed. So, what was the explosion for? "Tristan? Tristan?!" I shouted Tristan's name in the crowd. Everyone seems a bit confused and panicked. They keep running around, so I squeeze through them to make my way.

That's when I saw him, the boy that wears black jean with red strip collar shirt, along with black jacket! I quickly make my way toward him while running frantically.

"Thank goodness you're alright!" I said. Tristan chuckles slightly. "What made you so worry about me?" He then looks around. His brunette hair shines with the sunlight ray. It's gorgeous. His red eyes also shimmering. My heart starts pounding so hard upon seeing the beautiful face of his.

I love him.
I love Tristan.
I love this genius in front of me.
I love my cousin.

"I love you." Ouch! That snaps me!!!

Did he just say that he loves me? Or am I imagining things? Then, he embraces me tightly. That's—shocking me.

When he hugs me, I look around. What did the explosion was for? A blunt explosion?

"After this camp end, let's have a dinner near the river at your house. You remember that river, right? The river when you almost drown and I save you. Haha. That's the first time I get so close to you, you cling so tight on me that it's hurt a lot." I frown.

"We just got there, Tristan, a while ago." "Oh?" He frowned, trying to remember. I gape.

Oh my god! I spun around; just to see the '360' students playing happily like nothing happened. I saw Gwen. She comes toward me with a broad smile.

"Are you the new student who's enrolling in this camp? You can place yourself in that dorm." She showed me the wing building.

"Anyway, welcome to the summer camp, a camp where you can enjoy yourself without adult! Although it's only for 3 days, you can still enjoy yourself as much as you want."

Suddenly, I remember what Tristan had said when I got into his room before the night I found out about the base… *'If only I never learn about anything big,'*. My eyes blur with tears. This is the end, the end of 360. No one remember anything about this society. The lab where I had being drugged, everything, had turn into infirmary which helped injured students. And that's what Tristan meant by being honest with his feeling! He is no longer 360, and he is being honest with me. I am so happy to know about it; even I am no longer the leader. It's just like a burden had weight off my shoulder. I will no more lie, but it kind of fun after some time.

Olivia and Alex are the persons in charge of students, guiding them on how to use equipment. They still are genius, but they only talk about games, about the exam marks that they got at school, about how they win tournaments...

CHAPTER XXII

"Wow! Nice hit, Stellar!"

"Good job! You're brilliant!" I smile broadly at Tristan.
Everyone gets out of the rink and pat my head. "Nice shot."
"That's amazing move, Stellar."

Tristan brings me to a café nearby to celebrate my victory.
"This is lovely." "Yeah, it is." I look outside the window of the café.

It had been a month since the '360' had being destroyed. What perplexed me is no one ever remembers that '360' exist. That relief me a lot.

I had made a decision. I will no longer proceed with that crazy idea of my great grandpapa. Sorry, Henry. But, it just happened that you got the wrong person.

"Are you still studying?" "Yeah, for the coming exam." Tristan laughs upon hearing my answer. "I think you don't have to put so much effort. You already surpass your classmates in everything that you did." "Well, let me think about it. Are you telling me to give chance to my other classmate to get number one?"

This time, he laughs out loud. "You got me." He clicks his tongue. "I don't think I need to do that. I deserve the number." "Yeah… you deserve number one."

I toss my coffee with Tristan. "To the victory." "To the victory."

Somehow, when I toss, I accidentally look into Tristan's eyes. It's glowing red.

It's trying to tell me something that Tristan doesn't even realize it himself.

That's when I realize something that was about to change…

-THE END-